GRAVEYARD
SHIFT

HALF BAKED BEANS
PUBLISHING

GRAVEYARD SHIFT

Written by
MANISH MAHAJAN

HALF BAKED BEANS LITERATURE
e -mail: publish.halfbakedbeans@gmail.com

First Published by Half Baked Beans in 2017
Copyright © Manish Mahajan

I'm coming back
I will return
I'll possess your body
And I'll make you burn

I have the fire
I have the force
I have the power
To make my evil take its course

Iron Maiden

Dedicated to my father late Mr G.J. Mahajan. Maybe his spirit is reading these stories. I certainly would like to believe so.

Introduction

One of the most satisfying feelings for any author is when he sits down to write the introduction for his book. Thanks to the overwhelming love, jingoistic support and well-rounded appreciation that my first book 'The Disappearance of Tejas Sharma' received, here I am rejoicing with that double delight feeling – writing a preface to my second book!

While it is true that 'Graveyard Shift' is just a continuation of my literary journey which began with 'The Disappearance of Tejas Sharma' – same genre, similarly set short stories – that is where the similarities end. The stories in this collection tend to be much longer, typically averaging around 6K words or more. This means these tales have more depth and variety. This means I hope to keep the reader hooked on for a longer time as the plot deepens presenting intriguing twists along the way. This also means that I have deliberately kept the narration simple and conversational. So in a nutshell, I have attempted to deliver something different here.

Why did I call this collection 'Graveyard Shift'? The Graveyard Shift is a term of apocryphal origin which first came into print during the 19th century to describe the eerily quiet working hours from midnight to 8 in the morning. Indeed, a lot of the work on this collection has happened during the late night, and it is an interesting coincidence that there are exactly 8 stories here – one each for the hour of the Graveyard Shift!

In writing these stories, I have tried to follow the principle – variety is the spice of afterlife. Fear can come in different hues – spooky, eerie, bizarre, scary, terrifying and nightmarish. Each of these are different degrees in which we sense the supernatural. It is my hope that the readers will get to experience some of these varied emotions while reading these stories.

Out of the eight, there are two stories which deserve a brief mention, because they are quite different. The first one is 'The Appointment' which is a simple story narrated by way of a poem written with an 'aa bb' rhyming scheme. I am not a poet, neither do I understand poetry, but when this idea occurred to me, I accepted the challenge. Hopefully, it has come out well. If not, then please forgive me if I have done the fine art of poetry a gross injustice.

The second story I want to call out is 'Betal Pachisi', the legendary tale from ancient India about King Vikram and the wily *Vetal*. When I was doing my research for this book, I stumbled upon the original unabridged text, and I realized very few people would have heard of it! As a mark of tribute to Indian literature, I am including my adaptation of this epic tale in this anthology.

I wrote this book over a five month period in 2013 beginning with the unrelenting monsoons of August and ending with the approaching coldness of December. During this time, I had to juggle my life between imagining macabre thoughts, fathering an infant son and performing my official work with my employer. That brings me to the thank you part.

I am immensely grateful to my wife for permitting me leave of absence from my domestic duties which also means she is yet to read any of these stories. I am equally grateful and lucky to have found myself amidst a relatively calm period at work, thus giving me ample time to engineer the twists and turns in my plots. I am grateful to my publisher Half Baked Beans for their support. My heartfelt thanks to Mr Amarnath Mukhopadhyay for spending several sleepless nights editing the manuscript. Lastly, it would be unfair if I did not mention the labours of my friend Tejas Joshi. Thanks are due to him for his questioning comments.

I hope you enjoy this work. But hey let me offer a warning, don't get too scared, remember *Darna Mana Hai*. There is a dark shadow which lurks around you. It feeds on your fear. It is watching you, even as you read this!

Manish Mahajan

Reach me at www.goodreads.com/manizoya
Facebook: www.facebook.com/manizoya

CONTENTS

THE APPOINTMENT

It was a beautiful morning, the sun shining bright
When I sat in my garden, preparing to write,
Little did I know a dear friend would come calling
Just as the autumn leaves had started falling.

He was my dear childhood crony.
Grey hair, tall frame with a face so bony,
Many idyllic noons we spent angling by the streams,
Growing up as brats chasing foolish dreams.

He walked in with an expression very grim,
I was astonished he had grown so slim,
I offered tea, snacks, or that game of chess…
But he did not care any less.

He slipped in my hand a piece of paper
Having handwritten alphabets with a gradual taper.
A smile surfaced on his shrivelled lips,
But the melancholy it could not eclipse.

Before I could talk with persuasion and deft
He got up with a start and left,
Leaving with me that portentous note
Which I unfurled to check what he wrote.

I shall come at 9:00PM 20th May - it said.
My perplexed, but worried eyes read.
The appointment now just a week away,
From the time and date that was today.

And then came that abrupt news,
All my sanity and insanity I had to lose
When I was told of his shocking demise last night
From cardiac arrest aboard the east bound flight.

My god! Who was it then who had me called?

MANISH MAHAJAN

I now realized why he looked so appalled!
Late in that night, I tossed and turned on my bed,
I shall come at 9:00PM 20th May – hadn't he said!

The weather turned inclement as the appointment drew near,
But what was it that I had to fear?
I shared my dreadful thoughts with my wife,
And she turned pale and prayed for my life.

On the night of 20th May, we sent our kid away
To his friend at my neighbour's chalet.
Both of us trembled as the hour drew near,
And the full moon shone bright and clear.

The sound of approaching footsteps outside the door
Made my heart cold to the core.
In the very next instant, the doorbell rang,
I heard the humming of a tune, the one he always sang.

The revenant stood there laughing heartily at my horrified face,
He had kept his appointment cheating death's unforgiving embrace.
He walked in freely like he always did,
His pockets full of chocolates for my kid.

He instantly put our edginess and fears to rest,
With his characteristic aplomb and garrulous zest
He talked about life after and its unbound pleasure.
We realized death had yielded him bountiful leisure.

Very soon, our sides ached from boisterous laughter,
Hearing of dead maidens for whom he was sought after
We did not even realize how the hours flew by
And finally, my friend got up to say goodbye.

At the door, he smiled and said - My dear,
I shall come to thee same time every year
Provided no one else comes to know,
That I return from the dead just to say my hello.

GRAVEYARD SHIFT

And so he came every year on the said time and day.
We even stopped sending our kid away.
No one knew about this annual haunt
And thus my friend kept visiting on his nocturnal jaunt.

But they say even walls have ears...
To my dismay, the grapevine was with my peers.
They told their wives who in turn told their friends
I languished, is this how the appointment ends?

Alas! The spread did not halt,
Soon my house was under siege from a media assault.
I fervently prayed the doorbell would again ring,
And I would hear the humming, the tune he would always sing.

Years passed by but he never came back,
I sat all night listening for his footsteps on the dirt track,
I dearly miss my friend
Having lost him now to some folly I can never mend.

HONEY, 'M BACK!

"Leave your hands, Madam, leave your hands," the dark skinned tribal boy shouted. He wore a cheap looking blue vest which clung to his small, but muscular chest.

"What?" Riya shouted back, unable to hear anything over the deafening din of the roaring waterfall behind her back.

The boy gestured her to leave her hands. She understood and tentatively loosened her grasp on the abseiling rope, her legs securely pressing on the only available rock ledge jutting from an otherwise vertical cliff. Slowly, as she became more confident and composed, she threw her arms out and made a 'V' sign with her fingers, the thick hand gloves making the 'V' hardly discernible. The dark skinned boy clicked the shutter of the camera which sputtered with a burst of 8 quick shots. "Perfect shot Madam!"

Riya sized her progress. This was quite a formidable spot to rappel down, much tougher than the earlier rappels she had attempted. Dabhosa, a tribal village in the economically backward district of Jawhar –a city and a municipal council in Palghar district, had lent its name to this majestic waterfall, the only perennial falls in the state of Maharashtra. Falling from a height of over 300 feet, it sent cusecs of white frothing water roaring down the river valley. Such was the force of the torrent that it had created a deep crater at the base of the fall.

She was half way down now. The white misty spray from the waterfall had drenched her completely and stray strands of wet hair stuck to her face making her look like a water-nymph. She shifted a bit in her safety harness which clung around her shapely waist taking the full weight of her body, and then gently released the nylon cord, letting it slowly slip through her gloves. She slowly began to descend again, using her legs to grope for cracks along the moss filled slippery bluff.

From the top of the cliff, Ketan Godbole looked down at his young wife dangling precariously and waved his feeble hands joyfully. Riya looked up at the timid, shrivelled face of her 62 year old husband. She had already descended 150 feet from the starting point where Ketan and the boys from the Dabhosa Nature Resort's safety team were stationed. Her face changed colour and she said slowly but spitefully, hate laced in every word she uttered. "Go on smiling, you swine. You won't see tomorrow. I promise you won't." Her words got lost in the swirling wind. And then she laughed. A wicked, sinister laugh. The prodigious cataract thundered down with renewed ferocity, fed gluttonously by the unrelenting rains of the past few days. She knew this was the perfect setting to eliminate that old hag whom she called 'my husband'.

A hop, followed by a skip and then with a final jump she made it to the landing point. She waved triumphantly to the rappel instructor at the top and gestured him a 'thumbs up'. Ketan, who was standing beside the instructor, thought she had waved to him and he waved back eagerly. "The sod. Can't bear him any longer," Riya muttered.

The landing point was a good 200 feet below the picturesque sunset point from where she had begun her descent. The sunset point was nothing but an extension of a bend in the narrow, winding dirt road coming from the village leading all the way up to the resort, built on government land but run by a private operator. The government had agreed to this contractual partnership on the condition that the resort would employ locals, thereby helping the poverty stricken tribals.

It was getting dark and the party needed to pack up. The rappel instructor signalled the blue vested boy below with his hands indicating they would not pull up the ropes for the night. There was a group scheduled to visit the site tomorrow and they had asked for rappelling as their choicest activity. The boy waved back in agreement, and proceeded to remove the harness, helmet and gloves off Riya. Very soon, Riya was trotting along the narrow footpath covered with beautiful ferns on both sides, following the tribal boy up to the starting point, from where they would collect their bearings and head back to the resort for the night. It was a relaxing and easy uphill climb, however, her hyperactive mind did not allow her to soak in the pleasure of the beautiful landscape around her. Thoughts went on ringing inside her head. Thoughts of the old man she had married only for money.

It was exactly three months ago, they had met at an opulent evening party. Riya Solanki was dressed to kill, her svelte hour-glass figure attracting every man's attention like a fly to the candle. Her modelling career was in doldrums, the offers had been dwindling both in frequency and quality. She urgently needed money to pay off the debts which her wanton, profligate lifestyle had made her accumulate. That was the situation when she first met Ketan Godbole, the largehearted philanthropist, but more interestingly, the billionaire business tycoon. She had heard whispers in the crowd about Ketan having no heir as his first wife had died childless. Then and there, the devil in stilettos that was Riya, had plotted a cunning plan to marry this man. It had been fairly easy for the master seductress. After all, old men were very easy prey. In the next two months, the wedding bells had rung. Unheard by anyone, the silent death knell on Ketan had also rung.

Ketan coughed softly. The wind, rain and cold were getting to him. He saw Riya climbing up the hill and shouted to her in great appreciation, "Bravo, honey. You did it. I was scared when you took the first step off that cliff."

"What will you give me for this feat?" Riya demanded with childish joy as she ran up to Ketan and hugged him. He almost fell over.

"Diamonds…your favourite brand De Beers."

Riya tightened her embrace. Her arms dug into the flagging muscles on the old man's frail torso.

"No," she cried "All I want from you is this," she invitingly put her finger on her pouted fleshy red lips.

"Ha ha," Ketan laughed hoarsely and went into subsequent bout of coughing. "In the private confines of our room, honey, not here. Let's wait for the night. The waiting is fun!" He winked. Riya winked back. "Yes. Let's wait for the night."

They strolled back to the resort, hand in hand. By now the evening sky was overcast with dark clouds and rumbling sounds of thunder could be heard at distance. In a few minutes, they reached the resort entrance. Its massive iron gates had a signboard whose one hinge had come loose. The bold black writing on its white smudgy background had washed out and it appeared pale grey. Tree branches with thick leaf cover, dripping with rain drops, covered most of the signboard. When the wind blew aside the foliage, one could read: "Dabhosa Nature Resort. Private Property. Entry Restricted." The resort lay on the sloping terrain of a canopy covered hill overlooking the sylvan valley below, with eleven spaced out private cottages on the left side of the road. The dining and the recreation centre were on the right. Each cottage had a view facing the waterfall with a private attached balcony overlooking the gorge. Riya had booked a super deluxe cottage suite which was right at the end of a narrow cobblestone path that snaked across the resort property, threading the widely dispersed cottages. This arterial path had short, knee length shaded lamps installed at regular intervals which would daintily light up the place at night making the whole resort look magical.

"Hello sir, hello madam. Hope you've enjoyed the rappelling." The resort manager called out as he came running when he saw the couple making their way into the resort's reception lobby. He readily offered them two clean white linen towels.

"Yes, Ramesh. It was indeed a great fun. My wife managed to do it, but I was too scared to even look down," Ketan replied cheerfully. The grin on his shrunken face amplified the wrinkles.

"Madam is brave," replied Ramesh in an appreciating tone. "The incessant rains make it even more difficult to rappel at this time. We have had nonstop rains for the last few days, sir. In fact, the low bridge on the road from the village is overflowing. No vehicles can cross now."

"Oh! That will be disastrous! I need to get back to Mumbai tomorrow to attend some important meetings," Ketan said with a real concern.

"No worry, by morning the water level should subside. Sir, by the way, I got to leave now to catch the bus to town. Today, being Sunday, all the other guests have already checked out at noon. Apart from you, there is nobody staying here overnight."

"You mean we will be alone in the entire resort," Riya jumped in the conversation, her eyes gleaming with excitement.

"Yes madam, you have the whole resort for yourself. The dinner will be laid at 8:30 in the dining hall across the road," Ramesh gestured in the direction of the hall. "The cook and staff will also leave for the village. There will be just the watchman here, who sleeps in his small shaft by the dining hall."

"Fantastic." Riya's voice had an unexpected zing in it. "Absolutely perfect." She slipped her arm in Ketan's and said "Is it not perfect, sweetheart, just you and me in this desolate resort far away from everyone else! The rains have cut us off in this beautiful paradise."

Ketan coughed again. "Yes of course, honey. That's indeed amazing. But I am a bit worried about tomorrow. Hope we don't get any more rain tonight."

"Only if you live to see tomorrow, sucker," thought Riya.

'Minerva' - the super deluxe cottage which Riya had booked was Dabhosa Nature Resort's most expensive and marquee accommodation. It was a luxurious two storied suite fitted with designer décor and exotic looking interiors. Just outside the cottage's main door, two hammocks stretched invitingly above a well mowed private garden covered with aesthetically planted ornamental herbs. The suite had two impeccably furnished rooms on the ground floor and one small study above. A mahogany staircase with beautifully carved balustrades led up to the secluded attic like study above, which had a curtained glass wall on one side overlooking the waterfall.

"Honey, I need to finish some office work. Why don't you take some rest till dinner," Ketan said in a caring tone.

"Ok. I am really tired," Riya raised her hands, her fingers intertwined and yawned. She slumped heavily on the giant four poster bed which lay in the middle of the bedroom. The day's activities had tired her and she really needed to rest, before her homicidal agenda could commence. Ziplining, kayaking and then finally rappelling down that precipitous rock overhang had truly exhausted her. All through the day, her frail, faithful but foolish husband stood by the side-lines cheering her all along. Riya closed her eyes. She could hear Ketan moving in the study above as he set up his laptop and papers on the table. "Old poker face wants to work! What a shitload of man, anyone else would have pounced on me right away," she thought. Ignoring the noises from above, she let her thoughts drift away and fell asleep.

It was by sheer providence that Riya had come to know of this resort located about 180 km away from Mumbai. From the information she had gathered, it sounded just perfect, remote and secluded. She had been thinking over it since many days now. Within a few days of marriage, she had found the means to eliminate Ketan without any suspicions falling on her. Ketan was used to taking sleeping pills every night. An overdose would make it appear as a freak accident or suicide. As flawless the plan appeared, it proved somewhat impossible to execute. Ketan frequently remained away from home, always busy at work, travelling abroad most of the time. Lately he had been under tremendous pressure due to the falling share prices of Godbole Industries and spent most of his time either at office or at his personal office-chamber at home. Riya was as such unable to get close to him. Days rolled by and she was getting more and more impatient. Then finally this resort gave her an idea of frisking Ketan off on a private getaway. He also fell for the idea, deeply touched by his young wife's loving concern towards his dwindling health. The booking arrangements were made in no time, business schedules were re-arranged, deferred to accommodate this weekend outing and by Sunday morning, the couple left by road, headed for the waterfall. Riya had slyly insisted not to take the driver along and opted for driving the car. Finding her interest Ketan also agreed.

"Time for dinner, honey," He neatly arranged all the papers and rubbed his tired eyes. Then he walked up to the window and pulled the curtains apart. "Nice view," he muttered. An owl hooted at some distance and once again he called out, 'Riya, are you still sleeping? It's already 8:45, let us hurry before the staff leave without serving us dinner."

Dinner was uneventful and quick. Ketan ate heartily while Riya just took one bowl of mushroom soup and a chicken drumstick. The huge dining hall was empty, as they were the only guests left in the resort. After dinner, Riya lingered around to check on the movements of the staff. To her immense relief, she saw them leaving hurriedly after cleaning the kitchen. As one of them was passing by, she called out casually "Hello, can you tell me where does the night watchman sit? We are staying over in 'Minerva' cottage across the road."

"Are you asking about that drunkard, Ma'am? He can be found now in that tent over there drinking country liquor," the man said amusedly. "He would be of no use, Madam. Soon he would be totally drunk." With that, the man left.

Riya nodded with a smile and said to herself 'Excellent. In that case, he would not hear any cries for help tonight."

They came out from the dining area and sauntered along the dark road, saying all the coy words, playing all the passionate games that any newlyweds would. The mild drizzle, the darkness, the music of the crickets in bushes, the absolute privacy and the sounds of the night all around created a romantic ambience all around and added to their seductive fun. In no time, it began to rain more strongly and they got totally wet. They entered the lush green private garden of their cottage suite, falling over each other and finally climbed on a hammock, where they lay snuggled in the rain.

It was 10PM when they got down from the hammock and entered their cottage. Riya shut the main door and locked it securely. "Time for action," she thought. After changing her dress lovingly she shoved Ketan towards the bathroom for a hot shower, and then quickly ran up to the study. She took out a Tetrapak carton of milk from the refrigerator and poured it in a glass. Next, she quietly slipped in a dozen sleeping pills and stirred the milk noiselessly till those had dissolved completely. She carefully placed the glass beside Ketan's laptop and covered it with a plate. "All set now, good riddance Mr Godbole," she thought. She quietly came down the stairs, undressed and got in bed.

"Darling, let's make love. I have been waiting since morning," Riya called out to Ketan in a moaning voice which sent his senses in a tizzy. He was looking at the mirror, wiping his face.

Ketan turned and walked up to her recumbent body and smiled. "Did I not tell you the waiting is fun? Let me first finish the presentation which needs to go to the board of directors, and then I am all yours for the rest of the night."

Riya had the knowledge of Ketan's upcoming meeting tomorrow. As such she had anticipated such a response from him and that suited her plan well. Ketan softly kissed her on the cheek and walked up to the study. Riya called out from below "Darling, don't forget to drink your milk."

"Sure."

Ten minutes passed. Riya tossed and turned in the bed, waiting patiently. Another ten minutes also passed by but Ketan was still awake and working on his laptop. Riya was getting impatient. "Wish I could drown that tumbler down his bloody throat," she thought, her restless mind unable to stay calm any longer. She was about to remind him again when she heard a shattering noise from the study above.

"What happened, dear," she called and sat up on the bed.

"Nothing at all, by mistake my elbow hit the glass of milk and it fell."

"What!" Riya shouted. Disbelief turned to anger which she quelled from bursting, but she still could not hide her frustration. "Ketan, why are you so careless! There was just one pack of milk left in the fridge."

"Hey chill, no problem honey, I know you are very much worried about my health but I am not going to die if I can't have my milk tonight," Ketan laughed out innocently. His voice echoed down unknowingly mocking a seething Riya and infuriating her even more. She dug her nails into the mattress like an angry she-cat and viciously scratched the bed sheet.

For the next couple of minutes, Riya paced up and down in the room, her mind working furiously. "I cannot let this chance go by. He has to die. The bastard HAS to die." Still dressed only in her innerwear, a flimsy negligee, she stepped out on the balcony and stood with her hands resting on the railing, looking blankly into the dark abyss in front of her. The cold air and the roar of the waterfall somewhat soothed her agitated senses. Looking down into the darkness, she wished her husband was down there. Down there, his body crashing against the sharp rocks and swept away by the raging river deep in the forest, perhaps getting stuck somewhere downstream and rotting till the carrion feeding birds ate it away. Yes, down there, that was the right place where he should be.

"But how the hell do I get him out here and push him down," Riya thought. A lightning flared in the distance and briefly illuminated the countryside silver. Her eyes fell on a bunch of coir ropes lying in one corner of the balcony. She stared at them for a while and raised her eyebrows as a sinister plan hatched in her mind. An evil smile cracked on her lips. Quickly she unwound the rope and slid her fingers on it. Lying under the alternating effects of a scathing sun and fretful rain for a long time, the rope's fibres had rotten stiff and sharp; they cut into her fingers making her cringe slightly. "Nice, very nice, this would bury deep in that rascal's delicate old neck."

Riya instantly made up her mind and realized that there was no time to waste. She dashed into the room, slipped on a silk satin gown, straightened her hair and ran up to the study. Ketan looked at her and smiled. "Few more minutes, honey, by then it'll be over." Saying this Ketan turned his attention to the laptop screen again. Riya noticed that the carpet under the study table had a big damp patch where the spilt milk had seeped through. Hiding the rope behind her body, she silently walked up behind his chair and began to caress his wispy white hair lovingly.

"Coming, coming, won't take long. It should be over in 10 minutes, hon…" Ketan did not speak any further. A sudden stinging pain shot through his wind pipe as the rope constricted tighter and tighter around his neck.

"Yes, it won't take long," Riya yelled savagely, "I gave you the option of a painless death but you threw that milk away. Now go on bearing the pain, darling! It should be over in 10 minutes."

Taken by surprise, Ketan was dumbfounded and horrified. Impulsively, his hands bend back trying to repel Riya, but she was stronger and he was not in the best of health. Almost instantly, the coughing and wheezing set in. His legs kicked, making the litter bin below the table tumble. Riya ruthlessly put all her strength into her hands and yanked. The sharp edges of the rotten rope cut deeper into soft, tender flesh.

"Riyyyaa… whaaar…you….doeen."

"Die my darling, die die…so that this poor, young, weak widow can inherit your entire wealth," she said laughing hysterically.

Ketan was gradually losing his senses, numerous black rings began to circle in front of his eyes. He jerked his head violently from left to right causing the chair on which he was sitting to tip over. Both fell sideways, but still Riya hung on to the rope as tightly as she could. The fall's impact, however, loosened Riya's grip for a split second, and when she constricted the rope again, it did not entirely catch the neck but slipped slightly up towards the chin. Air now gushed into Ketan's lungs. He desperately fought for his life but Riya held on tenaciously, like a hungry lioness clinging on to a thrashing wildebeest's throat. Ketan's weak body was gradually giving in, she expected that, and she could sense it too. But Ketan was a wily, strong willed man. In utter desperation to remain alive, he somehow managed to thrust an elbow into Riya's face, lunged away from her and tumbled on the floor.

In that small study, both husband and wife lay sprawled out on the floor, nursing their respective wounds. However, the damage to the former was fatal. Ketan had a massive cardiac arrest due to prolonged asphyxiation caused by the constriction around his throat. For a few seconds, his gasping body shook violently. It would have ended this way for this poor, unfortunate man, but he did not escape his wife's savagery even in his last dying moments. Seeing her plan fail yet again Riya was now livid with rage. Every reason, logic and sense deserted her furious mind. She got up and snatched a knife lying near the fruit plate and pierced it repeatedly with brute force into her dying husband's heart, twisting it at each strike.

"Bastard," she screamed. "First you escape the sleeping pills, and then you escape the rope, now let me see how you live through this." With a delirious yell, she plunged the knife yet again into Ketan's blood soaked chest.

Ketan had died instantly at the very first stab, but she kept on impaling the sharp blade into his heart like a possessed maniac till her arm ached. She finally let it go, stood up in a staggering motion, wiping the blood off her face.

At the stroke of midnight, inside the study of that plush secluded cottage in the deserted resort by the thundering waterfall, Riya sat laughing triumphantly beside the dead body of her husband. She had done it. Ketan Godbole was dead. The bloody saga was finally over.

Little did she realize that her night had only just begun.

~~~

Riya woke up to the sound of the banging door.

After the murder, she had coolly planned to take an hour's rest before cleaning up the mess. At around fifteen minutes past midnight, she had crashed into the welcoming softness of the spring mattress after enjoying a hot shower in the bath. She had set the alarm for 1:30, but only after fifteen minutes' sleep, the front door's banging woke her up.

"I am certain that I had securely locked the door when we came in," she sat up in her bed, looked in the direction of the door and was astonished. It was open!

"How did it open by itself?" puzzled and a bit nervous, she got up. Half asleep, she walked up to the door, stopping by the bathroom to splash some water on her face. The coldness of water was stinging, but felt good. At the door, she stood looking outside at the dimly lit garden. It was raining heavily now. "Maybe I did not lock it properly and the wind threw it open."

Another disturbing thought clouded her face. "Did someone sneak into the cottage?" But she dismissed it outright remembering there was not a living soul around for miles except that drunken sleeping watchman. "Ok weeping widow, there is much work to be done. Wish I had brought the glycerine, how the hell am I going to cry all day when the world gets the news that Mr Ketan Godbole fell over the cliff and his body is missing," She laughed wickedly.

First on her checklist was cleaning up the ground floor. She had to remove any errant stains of blood and then dispose of the knife and rope, both she had brought down from the study. Getting rid of them proved to be easy, she simply tossed them firmly over the balcony. Erasing the proofs of murder in the two rooms on the ground floor, however, took a little more time than she had expected. When everything was done, she became satisfied and called out loudly in a mocking tone, "And now, the dead man deserves an honourable burial." Riya briskly made her way up the staircase. The moment she reached the landing of the study upstairs, a chill down her spine. She let out a scream.

Ketan's body was not there!!!

Fear now took its firm footing in her conscience and she looked again, rubbing her eyes. "Oh my god, did the bastard survive that stabbing as well? I was certain he was dead." She was kneeling down at the exact spot where Ketan was brutally slain. Dumbfounded she looked around the study room. Then she saw it. On the glass pane overlooking the dark valley, she saw the weak impression made by two thin hands, the right one slightly higher than the left. Riya gasped, horrified by the sight of fresh blood dripping slowly from the tip of each finger, creating ten scraggy lines that streaked down the glass pane. They had spelt out ten alphabets illegibly. Riya strained her eyes to make out what those letters read. It was difficult to read against the dark background of the night sky. Suddenly the countryside lit up with a distant flash of lightening and Riya read the message!

H...O...N...E...Y...... M...B...A...C...K

"Aaah," she screamed wildly. Tears rolled down her cheeks. "This cannot be. You are dead. DEAD." Her screams and cries echoed shattering the deathly silence of the study. Nobody except her dead husband would listen to her delirious crying tonight!

Riya suddenly remembered the open front door and it was clear to her now. No one had tried to break in the cottage, on the contrary, someone had calmly stepped out into the dark cold rainy night. That someone was her dead husband.

Just then the two hand impressions exploded and shards of the shattered glass flew in all corners of the small study, a few piercing Riya's delicate skin making her bleed a little. She yelled insanely and ran down the stairs, almost tripping over the last steps and darted outside the cottage. She paused to take her breath in the garden. It was not exactly pitch dark, those knee length shaded lamps were still glowing, but the unrelenting rain made visibility poor. The whole surrounding wore an eerie look. She had only dropped down on the grass, sobbing loudly when her gaze fell on the hammock. All on a sudden, it began to rock gently to and fro, just like it had when they had slept in it together. But this time the bulge in the hammock suggested only one person lay inside it. There was no room for the second person now.

"Please forgive me, Ketan, please," Riya wept, her gaze transfixed at the swinging hammock. There was no reply. By then the wind had picked up into a swift gale and the rain fell obliquely. Riya lay sprawled on the grass crying wildly like a frantic, thoroughly drenched to the bone. With all those bleeding cut marks on her body, caused by the shards of glass, she looked like a mad woman. Somewhere in the garden shrubs, a toad croaked fervently for his mate. Riya wept and wept, she had killed hers.

She got up after a while with a staggering movement and wiped her tears. "I accept my crime. Tomorrow morning I am going to hand over myself to the authorities and confess everything. Ketan, I am really sorry, please forgive me." This time too, there was no reply. The dead man's silence unnerved her even more.

A sudden sound made her alert. She saw footprints form on the sloshed muddy ground near the garden, just outside the cottage door. She cupped her hands over her agape mouth when she saw pools of swirling reddish water in the depressions made by those ghastly footprints. The footprints seemed to be heading away from their cottage towards the direction of the lighted cobblestone path that skirted the perimeter of the resort. Fearfully, she looked over her back to where the hammock hung. It had stopped rocking and lay perfectly still. Riya understood Ketan wanted her to follow him into the darkness. Determined to seek forgiveness for her crime,

GRAVEYARD SHIFT

Riya hurried out of the cottage's private enclosure and stumbled on to the lighted path.

"I need to find that watchman and wake him up. I will tell him everything. Maybe if there is a phone connection somewhere, he can call the police," she said to herself.

The path looked mesmerizingly beautiful in the wet night, but alas, its beauty was lost on the frazzled young woman who tottered along fearfully, in search of help. The path took Riya past three or four cottages; all of which stood dark and silent against the black sky, presenting grim, disapproving facades as if severely reprimanding her for her sins. She shuddered with the feeling of dread as she passed one dark cottage after the other. There was a sharp bend to the right, and thereafter the path climbed on the steep gradient of the hill. Riya turned around the bend and stopped in her tracks, when her eyes fell on the cottage which stood there. There were lights switched on inside.

"That is strange. I definitely heard the manager say that tonight the resort would be without any guests except us. Maybe someone did decide to stay over," Riya thought for a while, staring at this cottage which was much smaller and less furnished than their cottage. She slowly approached the cottage's front door, and was startled to hear muffled voices from inside. A sense of relief came over her, but she failed to observe it as odd that people would be chatting away such late in the night.

"Voices! People! Thank heavens, I must go inside and seek their help." Riya ran up to the door, hesitated a moment, but went ahead and rung the bell. There was no answer. She waited for some time more and pressed the bell again, this time a little more persistently. The murmurs continued inside the cottage, but no one came to answer the door. Getting a little impatient, Riya now gently placed her hand on the door and found it to be open. She pushed it and cautiously entered the cottage. This one's layout was a bit different, with a small waiting area and a master bedroom towards the left. The waiting hall was empty and the voices were coming from the master bedroom. Though Riya could not make out anything, the voices, however, sounded strangely familiar.

Puzzled, she peeped inside the bedroom. There was no one there! A wall mounted television with blurred picture was the source of the mumbled voices. "Hello is there any one here?" she spoke softly wondering if anyone was in the bedroom's attached toilet. Yet again, there was no reply. The cottage was empty, this was strange. A fearful thought occurred to her and she blurted out in a treble, "Ketan, are you around?" She closed her eyes and shut her ears with her hands, expecting some macabre response from someone, somewhere, but the only sound in the cold air was the hoarse, incoherent voices from the TV over and above the constant muted roar of the waterfall. She heaved a sigh of relief. She was about to turn and leave, when she recognized the voice coming from the TV. Her heart skipped a beat and mouth went dry. It was her own voice!

More perplexed than afraid, she slowly walked a few steps farther into the room and stared at the TV screen. At that instant, the door banged shut on its own. Riya screamed and began to wail again. She knew who had slammed the door shut. She looked fearfully at the TV screen, its image was grainy and the sound crackling. The screen was replaying the activities which she and Ketan had enjoyed earlier in the day. Riya burst out wailing in another avalanche of emotions laced with regret. Sobbing and clearing her snotty nose, she saw the scenes quickly roll by one after the other.

...kayaking near the river...afternoon tea at the tree-top observation podium ... the tribal boys from the village setting up the rappelling gear ... Ketan cheering and coughing ... the harness and helmet being secured ... Riya posing for the photograph ... the treacherous climb up the narrow path ... the cheerful manager talking ... the laptop in the study... the dinner laid out for them ... staff leaving hurriedly ...the walk back to the resort ... the swinging hammock ...

"Stop it Ketan, please, I beg you. Don't show these to me," Riya beseeched, her eyes now swollen red due to constant crying. "I don't want to see it, don't show it to me, Ketan," her words were no longer coherent due to the accompanying sobs and wails. "I accept my crime, Ketan, please don't show it to me."

... the accidental spilling of milk ... her fingers caressing Ketan's hair ... bodies falling down ... a rope cutting in flesh ... more struggle ... Ketan lying

prostate ... the cardiac arrest ... plunge of the knife ... again and again ... oozing blood and ...

"No...Nooo...Noooooo" Riya shrieked insanely.

...honey, 'm back ... out in the garden ... toad croaking ... bloody footprints ... the lights in the cottage ... voices, people ... the open door ... the empty bedroom ... the TV...

"STOP IT," Riya screamed madly. She picked up a flower vase placed near the side of the bed and threw it with full force. It smashed into the shiny TV screen causing deep fissure - like cracks spreading out in all directions. Riya was now panting heavily. She banged her head on the floor deliriously, all the while weeping inconsolably. Suddenly there was a crackling noise from the TV. With infernal horror in her eyes, Riya watched the splintered screen spurt back to life, its cracks making the pictures in the video appear more ominous than before. "Nooooooo," she continued with her wail haplessly and tried to get up and run, but she could not. She was held there, firmly riveted to that spot and unable to turn her eyes off the screen in that position. He intentionally wanted her to watch. Every single bit of it, slowly, one by one. Against her will, Riya watched horrified.

...the study room on the top floor of the super deluxe suite 'Minerva', still bloody and grotesque, was now claimed by the elements as rain poured in copiously through the shattered glass pane. The curtains were billowing up due to the howling wind. On the table, lay the laptop, its screen still open but gone blank. It suddenly lit up and the blinking cursor asked for a password to unlock the user account. Keys punched on their own and the password was entered accurately. The home page loaded and revealed a beautiful black and white image of Riya's youthful smile. The blinking cursor danced around a little and then a short pop up window appeared. The cursor slid down a bit randomly and stopped at 'New', immediately a second pop-up window opened to the right of the first one. This time, the cursor moved upwards decisively until the words 'Microsoft Office 2007 Word Document' were highlighted and finally a new word document lay open. Then the typing began. Riya could not follow the text, the fonts were too small. It went on for a harrowingly long time. Words were written, deleted and then re-written. Sentences were edited. 1 page, 2 pages and finally the typing stopped at the middle of the third page. The last

two buttons hit were Ctrl and S…

There momentarily appeared a grainy image on the TV screen as the scene changed. Riya watched dumbfounded, shivering to the core. She could now see herself on the screen and let out a wild shriek. She knew Ketan would now show her what would happen next.

…she got up from the bed. It was the same room as this one. The dishevelled bed sheet and blanket were soaked with crimson red. She bore on her face a mysterious smile, the vacant eyes not complementing the smile. She walked slowly as if in a trance. The doors opened noiselessly as if not wanting to impede her walk. She stepped out of the cottage into the inclement embrace of the torrential rain. Taking one step at a time, slowly, she headed on to the cobblestone path. As she passed each lamp, it flickered slightly but regained its original shine after she had walked past. She did not look left or right or up or down, she just kept walking, her weary eyes transfixed forward. Very soon she reached the massive iron gate of the resort entrance in front of the reception area. The gate-lock turned smoothly, old hinges cringed painfully and the gates opened obediently on their own, to let her pass through. She was now on the dirt path outside the resort…

Riya yelled out another volley of plaintive requests for forgiveness. She was terrified beyond her wits now. In spite of all her efforts to not look at the TV screen, he made her do exactly that.

…it was pitch dark outside the resort, the clouds and rain hiding the moon and stars. Despite the darkness, she walked on the path confidently. Soon she reached the sunset point, from where she had rappelled earlier that afternoon. She stopped at the edge and stood there perfectly still. Her blood soaked negligee clung on to her supple body. The wind had picked up now and blew strands of hair across her face. She looked down at the valley which appeared like a black mass of nothingness belching out a deafening noise…

There was a faint click and the screen went blank. "Honey, 'm back," a voice said joyously from the door. Riya screamed as she recognized that all too familiar voice. Her heart leaped into her mouth and hair stood up on her sweaty back. There stood at the entrance of the room, the grotesque cadaver of Ketan Godbole, with his arms folded, grinning at her. The horrific gashing wounds on his mutilated chest were clearly visible beneath his unbuttoned blood stained shirt. Ketan walked over to the bed and lay down on it, all the time wistfully eyeing his beloved wife. He pulled the stark white fluffy blanket over him and called out in a cheerful voice.

"That can wait, honey," he said, pointing his finger to the television screen and shaking his bony chin dismissively. "Not so soon, not so soon." He chuckled. "The waiting is fun, But first let us now do something which we missed out," he laughed. Riya broke down and folded her arms in prayer, ruefully begging for forgiveness yet again.

"Come, honey, let's make love." Ketan threw open his arms invitingly.

The lights gradually dimmed and the cottage plunged into complete darkness as Riya Solanki stepped into her dead husband's loving embrace, one last time.

~~~

Monday 11:37 AM

BREAKING NEWS: INDUSTRIALIST KETAN GODBOLE, WIFE DEAD

The ticker flashed by at the bottom of the screens. By now, all news channels had picked up the sensational story and were telecasting it nonstop. A spectacled, dirty looking journalist shouted into the mike, "I am now standing in front of the HQ of Godbole Industries. Mr Godbole, the famous business tycoon and founder of Godbole Industries, was found brutally murdered in a resort, apparently by his wife, who also took her own life after killing him. This is a mysterious happening. The police are investigating the case and have taken up the resort staff for more questioning. I have here with us Mr Joshi, who happens to be Mr Godbole's long-time friend and business partner. "Sir, can you ...

2:00 PM

According to reliable sources, Riya, the ex-model and wife, left a suicide note, typed out in Mr Godbole's laptop. We are trying to get a copy of ...

5:12 PM

And let me show our viewers again, behind me is the exact spot where Mrs Godbole, put the ropes around her neck and jumped down the cliff.

8:45 PM

We have DC (Crime), Maharashtra Police with us, "Sir, can you tell us something about the note left behind by Mrs Riya?"

"Sorry, I cannot share anything at this point."

Wednesday 10:00 AM

The police claim to have solved the case. The suicide note written by Riya, admitting her crime and explaining in sufficient detail why and how she did it, will be used as the prime evidence in this murder case. According to the police, what took them time is that they were baffled about one thing. There were no fingerprints of Riya on the laptop.

TALES IN THE TRAIN

After dinner, we started telling each other creepy tales.

It was not too late an hour actually to start a story-telling session, but since we were travelling in an overnight Express train, the usual tendency of the passengers there is to retire for an early sleep. One by one every light was switched off and the bogie fell into an unsettling darkness, lit only occasionally by streaks of light coming from halogen lamps of nondescript stations past which the locomotive thundered by. The elderly couple on the side lower and upper berths had also slept off and we just kept the dull blue night lamp in the passageway on. There were five of us in the partition of our reserved compartment. Mayank and I sat next to each other. I had covered myself in a warm woolly shawl and snugly rested my right elbow on the cold window ledge. Both the metal and glass shutters were down as it was a cold night. Next to Mayank sat the quaintly dressed old lady who had turned out to be a distant relative from his native village Pathrol in Bihar. There was a particularly striking fondness with which she had greeted and blessed Mayank when, in the general chitter-chatter that so characterizes long train travels, they had uncovered their respective positions in the far-reaching branches of the Prasad family tree stretching five generations. To me, it was a rather tenuous link, Mayank's father's first cousin's something-something, but seeing my husband elated at this chance meeting with someone he considered reverentially, I had willingly joined their conversation. Eventually when Mayank introduced me, the old lady or "*auntie*," as I had begun to call her in the course of our short acquaintance, showered me with equally copious benedictions.

"Aaah, my throat, it hurts," I wailed just loud enough for Mayank to hear. Since a few days I had this rather nasty and obstinate cough which refused to subside in spite of taking medications. I could have coughed without speaking, but the rhetoric was meant for extracting some gushing love and sympathy from my husband, but none was forthcoming, irritating me even more. "I wonder why you never fall ill," I said to him crossly "You would know then." He laughed at that and the twinkle in his eyes mingled with a caring smile made me forget my throaty discomfort.

Exactly opposite to me, next to the window, sat the fourth passenger; a good looking young man. I had been observing him keenly. He did not appear friendly and was busy with his tablet ever since he had boarded the train. Next to him sat the fifth and last traveller in our compartment, a garrulous cloth merchant from Agra who had introduced himself as Md. Ismail Sheikh. In stark contrast to his aloof neighbour, Ismail *chacha*, as I had begun to call him, had happily laid bare his entire life-history for consideration and opinions from his totally disinterested co-passengers. Through his nonstop rambling, I now knew how his brown leather wallet containing a princely sum of five hundred and twenty-two rupees was picked in the jostling crowd at Ajmer-Sharif; how his son was nearly expelled from school for picking up a fist fight with one of his classmates; then the rather pitiable tale of that young tea seller who unfortunately lost his eyesight and so on. All these ranged from his personal tragedies to the state of the nation, from the prices of fish to his views on the upcoming cricket series, he went on and on in an endless soliloquy which could have easily driven people sitting around him to the point of extreme annoyance. But I had taken a liking for Ismail *chacha*. He seemed to be an affable man with a big heart and often laughed at himself during his seemingly unending narratives, a quality which often was indicative of humility. It was Ismail *chacha* who had unintentionally veered the conversation towards spooky topics, probably inspired by the eerie setting created by the night lamp's blue glow above our heads.

"Does any one of you believe in gosts?" He had asked munching a juicy apple which had caused him to mispronounce ghosts. I must admit it was singularly the most appealing thing he had said all day, as everyone looked at him intently. Thrilled by this unexpected response from an audience who had otherwise summarily ignored him all along, Ismail *chacha*'s face lit up. "That's it," he exclaimed. "I am going to tell you a scary folklore from my native village in Uttar Pradesh," he resumed his monologue after what I thought was a hurried gnashing and a quick swallowing of the sumptuous looking apple.

"Have you ever heard of the legend behind the *Chhalava*?" he asked with gusto. Blank but intent stares from us meant no one had heard about it before. Ismail *chacha* beamed at us with the ecstatic look of a miner who had finally struck gold. Encouraged by our ignorance on the matter he continued "It is an age old legend about a spirit trapped between earth and hell. It is very popular in remote North Indian villages, like the one where I grew up."

For the next five minutes Ismail *chacha* took off on the tangent of his childhood village inundating us with uninteresting details about how many people lived there, what they grew in the arable land, why did the *Sarpanch*'s marriageable daughter run away with someone much to the dislike of her father and so on, till one of us gently reminded him about the *Chhalava*. With a childish 'sorry' he returned to the subject.

"A *Chhalava* is different from other types of ghosts. It will never attack its victim directly. It will first follow the victim, which may stretch even for months. There is a belief that during day time, it takes the shape of a large and ferocious ox. When it follows the victim, it gathers information about the voices of victim's family, friends and the victim himself. Finally when all is set, the *Chhalava* will confront the victim in the middle of the night by calling out to him in the voice of one of his family or friends. The key to escaping the *Chhalava's* deceptive call is never to look back. If the person looks behind, the *Chhalava* will challenge him into a duel which can last only till the first rays of the sun. If the victim loses, the *Chhalava* will rip him off into pieces. Though it is not possible to defeat the infernal beast, people believe the person who manages to overpower the *Chhalava* will be granted enormous luck for next seven generations."

Ismail *chacha* looked around at the wide-eyed faces of his audience with immense satisfaction. This was really creepy. I could sense everyone had been imagining their own versions of the legend in their minds. I was a bit startled when Mayank spoke out, "That is quite a frightful legend. But can you tell us about any real occurrence?"

"Oh yes, of course," said Ismail *chacha* emphatically. He animatedly narrated the real life experience of one of his maternal relative who had escaped from the clutches of the *Chhalava* and had become wealthy overnight. "And one more thing I forgot to mention," he said while concluding his tale. "The *Chhalava* is known to always haunt young bachelor men."

I don't know why but when he said that, everyone's curious gaze fell inadvertently on the only available bachelor in our group. I think he must have felt uncomfortable or afraid, and to my surprise, he spoke out for the first time.

"I have had a supernatural experience myself."

The train was slowing down and a big station was approaching. From the window along the side berths, I could see three or four parallel tracks gleaming in the powerful light of the lampposts of the station-yard. A couple passed our compartment noisily lugging their heavy suitcases to the exit area. It was most likely that they would be getting down at that station. I turned and looked at the young man, who had been waiting for everyone's attention. This story telling was turning out to be scarier than I would have wanted. I nudged closer to Mayank.

"It happened to me a year back but the memory is still very fresh. I was just out of college and working as a sales officer with an auto ancillary company. The work required me to travel almost constantly and I used to literally live with my suitcase, always readily packed. It was Diwali time and the hotels everywhere were running full. I had reached Igatpuri, a new town in my tour-list, quite late at night and wanted to be in bed as soon as possible. I hired a cab from the railway station and asked the driver to take me at an earliest to Shriram Country Lodge, where my company had booked a room for me. On reaching there I left the cab after handing over an additional tip to the driver and headed straight for the reception counter. However, there occurred a problem. The half-asleep man at the reception told me after checking the booking register that there was no booking in my name. After a lot of argument, he agreed that there had been a goof up at their end and they had allotted my booking to someone else (probably at higher fare due to the festive season). Finally, we settled the matter and the man offered me an alternate room. Having no choice otherwise as it was quite late in the night to find another hotel, I accepted the alternate arrangement."

"Now this was a rather big room with two separate single beds. It was very dingy and dusty, clearly indicating that no visitors had occupied it since quite some time. I waited patiently as the man and a helper boy cleaned up the place rather hurriedly. When they were finally finished they left with a weird expression on their faces, which now in hindsight I understand."

"I threw my bags on the floor, switched off the not-too-bright fluorescent lights and without changing my clothes, as I was feeling too weary, slumped on the bed. The mattress was very hard, not at all comfortable and exuded a strange horrid smell. I cursed my luck and made up my mind to get out of this hotel positively at the crack of dawn. They had been considerate in giving me a blanket which was big enough for me to even tuck its one end under my legs and still have lots of cloth to cover my head. Of course, it was smelly and dirty but being quite exhausted and thinking that I needed to stay here for a single night only, I chose to ignore those encumbrances and closed my eyes."

"I do not know how long I was asleep, but a strange noise woke me up. I looked at the luminous dial of my wrist-watch. It read 2.30 A.M. The noise was coming from the attached bathroom. At first I dismissed it thinking that rats might be having a merry time in this squalid place, but gradually with the passage of some more minutes the noise sounded more like a faint whisper. You would think why I did not ignore it, but for some strange reason it got into my head and was turning to be very annoying. Finally, I got up to check the source of the noise. When I peeped into the bathroom and switched the lights on, there was nothing! The noise had stopped. I can very well remember that I was extremely irritated. Just then, I heard a loud noise from the room. My heart beating fast, I looked back and in the dim light of the green night lamp I could see one of the lower drawers in the decrepit wooden shelf under the wall mounted mirror had slid open by itself. When I reached the shelf I was surprised to find a diary in that opened drawer, its pages open as if inviting me to pick it up and start reading."

The young man had a sudden hiccup and started coughing. Ismail *chacha* promptly handed him a bottle of mineral water. I saw Mayank's aunt pull out a shawl from her duffle bag and wrap it around her thin shoulders. It was a welcome pause for everyone to reflect upon what they had heard till now. The story so far had already freaked me out and I wished it would end soon. After gulping down the water, the young man felt relaxed and began talking again.

"Where was I? Yes the diary… well, I switched on the main lights and picked the diary up. Now I cannot recollect exactly what its contents were, but I will give you the gist of it. It was a diary maintained by a young man. There were random entries about the usual details of his day to day life and as such failed to create much interest in me. I was about to toss it back into the drawer when I noticed some dried blood marks on a couple of pages. And then, on the very next page I came across a brief suicide note. I can't recall the details like why and how and who he held responsible, it's been a year and I have tried to forget that unsavoury night all this while, but the one thing which really freaked me was his decision about the place of that suicide. He had mentioned he was going to end his life in that very room of the lodge. I was so scared, believe me, I shut the diary and with trembling hands shoved it back inside the drawer. I jumped onto my bed and covered myself completely with the blanket from head to toe. I cannot explain to you here how the rest of the night passed. I swear I could feel the presence of the dead man's spirit in that room. Sometimes it passed under the bed, sometimes it went into the bathroom and started letting out those awful noises. Once I thought I almost felt something heavy resting on my legs making them numb and immobile. I was so scared and frightened that I could not even utter a single word. I tried to scream but my voice did not come out, as if gagged by that invisible spirit. In hindsight, it appears silly why I did not run away at that very moment. Frankly, I cannot say."

The young man stopped speaking and looked around at the ashen faces of his four listeners. I don't know about the others, but I must confess that I had goose bumps all over my body. This was really one scary tale. It was Ismail *chacha* who was the first person to break the hauntingly eerie silence "That was indeed a terrifying tale, my young friend. But what happened next, did you manage to get out safely in the morning?" I was actually curious too and felt glad that he had asked what happened next. I, however, reasoned that it must have turned out all right. After all the young man was hale and healthy sitting with us here in the train. Yes, for sure, I wanted to hear this dreadful tale to its happy end.

"Well, there is not much more to say about how I spent that night. Though I was shaken and disturbed, I could manage to get some sleep and dreamt of a man inside that room with blood dripping from his mouth. He was tearing the pages of the diary and eating those one by one, all the while fixing me with a menacing stare. I have never been so pleased when I heard a cock nearby announcing the arrival of dawn with its loud voice. Hesitatingly I peeped out from under my blanket and looked through the glass panes of the window. The darkness of the night was gone but still the rays of the sun had not appeared. By now, all those noises and spooky sensations had ceased. With immense courage I sat up on the bed and looked around the room. It was perfectly still. The bathroom door was open and the light was still on. I waited for 10 minutes and when nothing awkward happened, I quickly picked up my bag and dashed out of the room. In my haste I did not notice that I had forgotten my cell phone. Down at the reception, I could find the hotel manager who had just woken up. Grudgingly I told him what had happened in the room last night. His response shocked me all the more. He mentioned there was no wooden shelf or diary in that room at all! Now this freaked me out completely. I yelled at him that I was getting out of this cursed place now and forever. He did not say anything to that, and asked me to wait while he started preparing the bill. Just then the young attendant who had helped clean up the room last night came running and handed me the cell phone. He said in a panting voice, "Sir, you forgot this, it was lying on the bed near the door. I was startled to hear this, and replied that I did not even touch that bed. In fact, I had slept on the other bed by the side of the window and not on the one near the door. On hearing this, the expression on the boy's face turned grave, he muttered in a shaky voice – "Then it must have been the ghost who slept there. The bed sheet is all crumpled and the blanket is lying on the floor." You see, I was absolutely in no mood to corroborate this. I had had enough. I just slammed a thousand rupee note on the reception counter and immediately left, without even bothering to collect the bill."

We all fell silent. The train was still at the same station. A tea vendor calling *"Chaaai...garam chaai,"* in a rather croaky voice stopped at the open window by the young man's seat and peeked inside expectantly. It was just the right booster we could have asked for.

"Tea anybody?" Mayank asked getting up and got thankful nods from everyone. One at a time, the young man took the flimsy plastic cups brimming with the hot beverage from the vendor and passed it to all of us. The tea was hot no doubt but woefully insipid. Its opportune and timely arrival, however, had done the trick and lifted our shaken spirits.

"I have some salted groundnuts," Mayank's aunt said cheerfully. "We can munch them and sip the tea while we talk."

"That was indeed some story. Phew! I was scared listening to it, can't imagine how you managed to spend the entire night in that haunted hotel room," Ismail *chacha* said between eager slurps of the tea. All of us vented out exclamations and expressed our genuine shock. The young man added a few more finishing touches to his extraordinary tale. For a brief moment, I wondered if this was all an elaborate lie which he had cooked up to amuse us. Ismail *chacha's* baritone voice interrupted my thoughts.

"Let's move on. It's your turn now," he remarked looking at me. "Me?" I asked. I was genuinely startled. This casual conversation which had begun so idyllically had now evolved into that boring each-one-tells-a-story game and I reckoned my number had come due to our seating arrangement. "I don't have any story to tell," I said shyly "I am so afraid of these things." I looked at Mayank and gave him that 'support me' look. To my dismay, he joined in the opposition ranks "Oh come on, don't tell us that in your 24- year life you have not heard or seen any weird happening? Why don't you tell them about that Metro station incident in Kolkata?"

With such a credible preface coming from my own husband, there was no way I could wriggle out from this now. I persisted with my increasingly weakening defences – "Oh! nothing happened that day, it was just an insignificant experience!" "I am not at all a good story teller," "I don't remember most of the things now," but all those weak excuses on my part proved to be futile, met only with an exhortative clamour of voices. I was rather compelled to give in and before beginning my story gave Mayank that obligatory glare which he must have understood as – "let's go home and then we will talk over this."

I pulled up my feet and sat with my legs crossed. The horn sounded and the train was on its way again. With all set, agog eyes of the listeners watching me, I began my tale. "Well, as you all might know there is an underground Metro railway system in Kolkata. The event what I am going to tell you now happened when I was doing my engineering in Kolkata. We used to stay out late and often had to rush to the station to catch the last train. It was on one such rainy monsoon night when I and my friend Sudha were returning from a late night party. We rushed to the nearby underground Metro station, I don't exactly remember which one but it was one of the important city centre stations and nearer to the place where he had our party." The young man suddenly interrupted, "Madam, can you tell me the location of the party you referred to just now? I have lived in Kolkata and remember the names of all the Metro stations. I hope, I can help you."

I was elated. It meant that he was listening to my story with great interest. I answered, "Oh, the party was at Camac Street, at one of our friend's residence." The young man instantly spoke out, "Then it should be the Park Street Station." "Oh yes, now I remember, it was Park Street, thank you" and I continued further. "We escaped the time wasting hazard of standing in the queue to buy our tickets as both of us, being regular commuters, had the smart card. Descending the underground flight of stairs in a hurry we quickly boarded the last train which arrived at the right time. I had, however, noticed that Sudha for some strange reasons had been very restless since we had left the party. I did not question her about that thinking she must be worried about getting admonished from her parents for being out so late."

"It was the last train on that route and we were really lucky to catch it. It was more or less empty. The carriage we boarded had only about ten passengers seated widely apart. Sudha and I were sitting near the sliding door. By then Sudha's restlessness had become almost hysterical, as she sat clutching her hand bag in an awkward way with her eyes shut tight. I asked her a couple of times whether everything was ok, whether she was all right, but she only gestured in a way by which I could not understand whether she meant a yes or no. I left her at her thing and took out the book I was reading. We must have been coasting along for a good 10 minutes. When the train approached the second last station, suddenly there was a violent rattling as if something was shaking the carriage. It was quite unsettling. At this Sudha went berserk and let out a shrill scream startling the other passengers. But nothing adverse really happened, the shaking stopped immediately and as usual, the doors slid open silently when the train halted at the station. A few passengers got down, no one got in and we were on our way again. Once more, just as the train was leaving the station-platform, we experienced that violent shaking. I must say it felt like an earthquake and I too began to feel uneasy. But like before, it subsided as soon as the train picked up speed and left the station behind. In another couple of minutes, our destination came and we got down."

"I was quite shocked to see Sudha. She looked like someone who had been through a terrible experience. She was sweating profusely but appeared much relaxed now. While on the escalator leading to the exit, I got her to speak up what was it that was troubling her so much? Her explanation left me stunned and I remember that time I felt quite scared too. She said to me – "*Arre* idiot, don't you understand, that station was Rabindra Sarovar! Doesn't it ring a bell in your head? When I confessed my ignorance she divulged that the particular station was notoriously famed, a haunted one and nicknamed 'Paradise of Suicide'. Most of the deaths reported on the Metro tracks were people who committed suicide at that particular station. Passengers who board the last train have had plenty of eerie experiences and even seen ghastly shadows. Sudha went on to say that on a particular night while she was travelling on board the last train and there was nobody inside the carriage, she could hear unearthly voices. Then another friend of hers actually saw an angry face staring from outside the window and trying to break it open!"

When I stopped my narration and looked around I could see pallid faces of my visibly shaken audience. I was feeling quite pleased with myself. And then, before anyone could react, something so extraordinary happened that it drove us to our wit's end. The old man who had been sleeping peacefully on the side berth suddenly sprang up and began to blabber some incoherent words. He also started making strange shaking movements with both his hands. He jerked his head in an abnormal manner from one side to the other. With the five of us already under the influence of fearful thoughts and frightful visions, the old man's unexpected and weird behaviour was enough to freak me out. It gave me such a jolt that I let out a wailing, piercing-scream. Five minutes of complete pandemonium followed. More shouts and cries were heard, all the lights were hurriedly switched on, Ismail *chacha* spilled the groundnuts on the floor, passengers in adjoining partitions of the compartment woke up, a baby started crying somewhere, and the old man's wife got down hurriedly from the side upper berth and began to comfort her husband. When Mayank inquired with her, she informed with an apologetic and embarrassed expression that it was nothing to worry about, just a seizure which the old man often experienced. It took some 10 minutes more for the seizure to subside and the man to lie down peacefully again. In the meantime, a few of us visited the bathroom, and when finally normalcy had set in and lights were switched off once again, we had shuffled our seating positions. I was still where I was sitting earlier, with Mayank beside me. Ismail *chacha* and the young man had interchanged their places. The old woman now sat opposite to us beside the young man.

"My god, that old uncle gave me the fright of my life," the young man said and we all laughed heartily. Then we talked a bit about my story about the Rabindra Sarovar Metro station. They asked me about the violent shaking before and after the train had left the station and I added a few more details which I could remember and then I said resolutely "Ok Mayank, the ball is now in your court."

I was actually quite eager to hear what kind of story my dear husband would tell. We had known each other for only a few years, and this topic of ghosts and horror had never slipped into our rather lovey-dovey courtship talks. So I was really curious.

"Hmm, yes it is my turn," Mayank said. "I have been thinking about what to share. You see, frankly, I have never had a supernatural experience myself so cannot relate any stories but I have heard a fair bit of folklore around *chudail*s from my native village Pathrol in Bihar," Mayank paused and looked at his aunt at the mention of their village. I had also turned my eyes on her when he had mentioned Pathrol, and noticed she became quite excited. I observed her closely and sensed it was not the mention of the village which had pleased her so much. It was the topic which Mayank had chosen. She nodded her head vigorously as if extending full support to Mayank in his narrative in case he forgot any titbits.

"*Chudail?*" the young man asked, "Do you mean *Daayan?*"

"The Indian witch!" remarked Ismail *chacha*.

"Yes, each region in India calls the witch with a different name. My Maharashtrian friend once told me his native village was under the spell of a *Hadal* which is the Marathi name for a witch."

"And I have heard that people in the hills and mountains of the north describe these creatures by the name *Picchal Pairee*."

"In the south, they have several names as well."

"Wow, then the Indian witch is truly a national phenomenon," a wave of light laughter among the group followed this comment.

Mayank then adjusted his posture which annoyed me a little, as he had moved a bit away from me. A part of me was eagerly waiting for this creepy session to end soon. I was glad that just two more stories were remaining. I pulled the shawl closer to my body and turned my face to listen to Mayank.

"Indeed there are several variants and formats of the Indian witch, but they are similar in some ways. Let me share with you the myths and folk tales I heard from my elders about the *chudail*s of our place. Now, for those of you who don't know, a *chudail* is basically a feminine spirit which is unusually hideous and terrible in appearance. She is supposed to have long sagging breasts and dishevelled hair. A common belief is that she has her feet backwards from which the term *Picchal Pairee* comes about; *Picchal* meaning backwards and *Pairee* meaning feet. Also she may have claw like hands and no mouth." Mayank raised his hands and formed a claw like figure and cupped his lips to demonstrate what he had just described. I felt this horrid illustration was entirely unnecessary, as the verbal description itself was disturbing. He could not read my mind and continued.

"But perhaps the most interesting superstition about a *chudail* in the first place veers around a relevant question. How does she come into existence? It is believed that she takes that form when a woman dies in childbirth due to negligence of her relatives, and decides to return in order to seek revenge. Filled with vengeance and fury she picks out the youngest male in the family and turns him into an old man by sapping his youthfulness. Her thirst for blood still not satiated, she turns on to other members of the family."

"How dreadful! Is there any way one can protect himself from a *chudail*?" the young man asked when Mayank had paused and looked around. For a brief moment, I thought he was inquiring for himself!

"Oh yes, that is also an elaborate affair I believe," Mayank said. "The helping hand of my grandfather's farm had once told me many tales related to *chudail*s and according to him the safest approach was to prevent the creation of one in the first place. Women who die in childbirth were sometimes buried face down instead of the usual Hindu custom of cremation. This is believed to be the best measure to prevent the formation of a *chudail*."

There was silence for a brief moment. The train was passing over a truss bridge and the clattering noise made the voice of Mayank quite inaudible. That brought out a halt in the conversation. I made up my mind that I had had enough for a night and was about to speak up with a suggestion of concluding our spooky session when the old lady exclaimed in a dejected voice.

"Oh no! Not all *chudail*s are bad."

For some reason, my tired mind was finding this old woman with a tenuous claim of blood relationship with my husband very irritating. "Maybe she is herself a witch," I said to myself spitefully.

"He he he," she laughed in a way which seemed very unnatural to me. I could not see any point in that annoying rhetoric laughter and impulsively felt my dislike towards this woman grow manifold. "My turn now. The last tale in the train. I will recite a true story about a *chudail* called Ratna from our native village Pathrol. Only this *chudail* was not at all nasty, neither terrible nor harmful." she said pointing her outstretched fingers at us. I observed her hand closely. In her I was trying to see any claw shaped sinewy fingers or deathly white skin but was disappointed. As much as I would have liked it, she was very much human. She began her tale of the Samaritan witch called Ratna.

"This thing, as I have already mentioned, is a true story witnessed by me. It happened some 30 odd years ago. I was then young and a hardy woman. You would imagine those were the dark ages for the villages of Bihar. Immense poverty, no medical care, unhygienic conditions, no electricity or water, frequent outbreaks of epidemics and a society steeped in ridiculous superstitions and beliefs. Practices like animal sacrifice to appease the gods were common. Black magic was a very real phenomenon and priests used to wander from village to village looking for ignorant grief stricken superstitious people who often needed their occult services to stave off several types of problems and adversities."

"Ratna was a simple, coy girl, having dark complexion and a frail body. She had long black hair which she generously oiled and plaited into two parts. There was nothing special about the girl. She was a typical village girl. However, she was a very loving and caring person especially towards children. In fact, when she was in her late teens, women with infant babies or toddlers used to conveniently call out to Ratna for looking over their kids while they ventured out into the farms to toil with the men. Thus she was looking after those children like what happens in a modern crèche. Life was tough in those years and women worked twice as hard, not like the young girls of today."

GRAVEYARD SHIFT

I was not sure if that was a thinly veiled attack on me. If she had thrown even a casual glance in my direction I would certainly have objected to her painting all modern girls with the same pre-conceived brush. But she just continued with her story and I ignored that unacceptable comment towards the larger interest of the intently listening group.

"Sometimes Ratna had up to 5 children in her care but she never complained or cribbed. Not once did I ever see her scold or speak harshly to any child. She genuinely loved children. However, God had planned a tragic future for such a benevolent girl. Ratna was an orphan who lived with her frivolous and uncaring uncle. When she came of age, her unscrupulous uncle sold her off to a well-to-do family as the bride of a sixty year old man. The family of her husband desperately needed a male heir and Ratna had to bear him a son. But the misfortune of the girl, years went by but she did not conceive. Poor girl, she was called names, sneered at and some women even stopped sending their children to her. Her in-laws also started treating her with contempt. It must have been terribly hard for her. But then finally, after six years of marriage, when her husband had already brought another seemingly fertile and younger girl home, Ratna found out one fine morning that she was expecting."

"It was a momentous and joyous occasion for the household. Everyone started celebrating and for the next few months, treated Ratna like a queen. Of course, there were the eternal pessimists who would not fail to jump on any opportunity to remind Ratna that she still had to deliver a baby boy. Things went on fine till about the seventh month of her pregnancy, when suddenly one night Ratna woke up writhing in pain. They got her checked by the local midwife who declared there was nothing to worry. The next day Ratna was feeling all right but this episode was the start of the inexorable misfortune of that poor girl. The family got scared and being highly superstitious considered the onset of pain as a bad omen. They called the local priest who incidentally also indulged in practicing black magic, and this horrible man announced that Ratna was bearing the devil in her womb! He totally brainwashed the family into accepting that the baby should be killed instantly on its birth."

"Now no one really knows what happened, but tragically one week later Ratna was found dead. The family hushed up the incident and refused to let any talk about this spilling out in the village. We all suspected that the poor innocent girl who was bearing a perfectly healthy baby in her womb was murdered, but the powerful and influential family managed to quell all suspicions. However, they still could not escape from one important consequence of their actions. They all feared Ratna would now turn into a *chudail* and seek revenge. And that is exactly what happened, at least in the first part."

"They did take all precautions though, which Mayank earlier mentioned, to prevent the deceased soul of Ratna getting transformed into a *chudail*. However, it did not work. When the first reports of her sightings came in, the villagers were obviously terrified. The family hastily ordered the erection of a stone structure outside the village lying in the path of the forests where Ratna and her unborn child were buried. Such a structure supposedly offered protection and prevented *chudail*s from entering the village. Do you still remember the stone ruins Mayank?"

There was a brief pause before Mayank answered. "Oh yes I remember, it was a Stonehenge style structure, massive rectangular slabs of coarsely cut stones erected in a circular shape. I used to often play there with other kids of the village. Wow, during my childhood days I always wondered who built that and why!" The lady smiled back nodding her head and continued.

"It was the year of the worst cholera epidemic I have seen in my life. Scores of people, especially the children fell victim. Village after village came under the unrelenting grip of that deadly disease and infant mortality shot up. Babies began to die. Lack of proper hygiene led to severe contamination of all sources of drinking water, there was no easy access to clinics and stubborn reliance on traditional and unscientific first aid methods resulted in the epidemic fanning out at an alarming rate. The villagers cursed their luck; as if the cholera was not enough, when a new problem in the name of Ratna had surfaced."

"No fortifications or stone structures outside the village limits could stop Ratna. Children saw her frequently, whom she tried to accost. Unfortunately even after death, she was misunderstood. As you will see later at the end of my story, she never meant to harm the children at all, but the villagers thought otherwise. They read the situation as awfully ominous. And then, one night, their fears turned true. In one of the houses, an infant had been born. He was then only a month old. Ratna stormed into that house in the night. She snatched the baby and headed for the deep forest which was believed to be her abode after her death. Next morning the villagers went berserk with fear. They made a thorough search in and around the house, but all their efforts proved to be futile. The frightened villagers finally started suspecting Ratna behind the sudden disappearance of that baby. In their mind rested an age-old belief that *chudail*s were used to feeding on new born babies to keep themselves young and healthy."

"How gruesome," I exclaimed. I was really tired now and this morbid story of a seemingly good witch was not turning out to be nice at all. I finally spoke up. "I am feeling really sleepy."

"Oh yes, it is getting late now. We should all sleep soon. Let the last tale get over, I am really curious to know what happened next," Ismail *chacha* replied summarily quashing any hopes of the session wrapping up early. I yawned and sleepily gave an unconvincing nod which at least had the desired effect on the raconteur, as she promised to wrap up her narrative in the next few minutes.

"That was not all. The very next night, Ratna did the same thing once again. She took away another baby, this time a two month old girl. There was complete panic and terror among the villagers. Finally the village head decided to seek help from *tantriks* so as to exorcise Ratna once and for all. They sent search parties to scan the forests but returned without success. However, they did find something disturbing. Ratna's dead body was missing from the grave where they had buried her! Every day at the crack of dawn, some fifteen or twenty men, armed with weird looking wooden staffs, their torso painted with symbols, went in search of their quarry. A couple of days passed, by now the hopes of finding the missing babies alive had faded. It was assumed Ratna had eaten them. The families, especially the heart broken mothers, were inconsolable. It was only when the village team decided to take the risk and venture into the forest at night that they finally tracked her down."

"Now I don't really know what happened as I was not a part of this particular expedition. I am just repeating to you the story that went around in the village. The night party found an abandoned old barn deep inside the forest, probably built for some storage purposes by the forest department. They found Ratna just outside its door, immediately caught her by her hair, and dragged her mercilessly into a clearing some distance away. The exorcism rituals lasted a couple of hours and by midnight, they had expelled her spirit. The party had just begun celebrating when suddenly someone heard cries coming from the barn. They ran towards the barn and when they entered it, they were shocked at what they saw. There, in front of them, lay the two babies on a bed of dry twigs and hay, perfectly fine and suckling their thumbs."

"So that was it, Ratna was never seen after that. Although she was despised and loathed, most people realized that Ratna had actually saved the babies from a certain death. During that year, I recall, all infants succumbed to the cholera epidemic, only these two babies survived."

"Incredible. It is unbelievable that a witch cared for the babies. Hard to believe it is true," the young man said.

"But I did not understand one thing," it was Ismail *chacha*. "How did the infant babies survive for over a week with a witch like Ratna?"

"Ha, that is indeed the puzzle which no one will ever know. Perhaps one of the survived babies can answer that question." the lady said with a mischievous twinkle in her eyes.

"Mayank, would you tell us what did Ratna feed you?"

I must admit here that I have never been so shocked in my entire life. That one statement caused a hushed uproar amongst us. Amidst exclamations and low whistles, everyone stared at a totally dumbfounded Mayank whose mouth was agape with utter astonishment. I could see from his expression that Mayank was equally stunned at this revelation and totally at a loss to give an answer as he had no prior knowledge. Stammering a bit, he told us his parents had died when he was only 3 years old and then his paternal uncle's family has adopted him so they would naturally not know about this incident.

"And my dear child," the lady looked at me with a broad smile "that could also be the reason why your husband never falls sick!"

The train was slowing down. The young man yawned and peeped outside the window. Another station was due to approach within a few minutes. He got up and stretched his aching limbs. "Folks that was a wonderful session of storytelling. Time to sleep now." Everyone agreed and one by one each one of us retired for what remained of the night. I lay awake for a while, still wondering about the last tale. But very soon, as the train began to move again and gathered speed, the monotony of the clickety-clack sound rising from the movement of the wheels hitting the metal tracks created an effect of sweet lullaby and I finally fell asleep.

A Night in the Hastings House

"But why Hastings House?" Shibashis asked.

Rimli hastily pulled out a paper from her folder and read it out aloud:

"When Warren Hastings, the first Governor-General of British India left our shores in 1785, he, or those who had packed and shipped his belongings, misplaced an old black bureau which contained some prized papers and miniature portraits. There is plenty of evidence that this loss actually occurred and that it caused Hastings much concern. According to folklore, the ghost of the Governor-General comes at midnight on New Year's Eve every year to the portico of the Hastings House in a coach driven by four horses. After getting down from the coach, Warren Hastings rushes up the staircase in search of the lost documents. It appears that in the impeachment proceedings of Warren Hastings by the British Parliament in the late 18th century, these documents would have been of great use to the former Governor-General to prove his innocence."

"Is that what you found on the internet?" Shibashis Haldar asked sceptically. He was smoking a Gold Flake and pensively blowing out concentric circles of smoke. As the head of the Kolkata chapter of the newly formed organization 'Ghost Hunters of India', Shibu-da, as he was fondly called, was responsible for coordinating and commissioning all the activities of the group. Today the small team had assembled to discuss a proposal and essentially secure his affirmative nod.

"Yes sir, I have sourced that information from online research," replied a flustered Rimli. She was only 18 and a new volunteer who was yet to understand the exacting standards of Shibashis.

"Sorry, I cannot commission a project just on the basis of some online research. Need more solid matter with concrete justification," he waved his hand dismissively and turned his back. Rimli looked at Tapas who nodded at her reassuringly. Now Tapas interjected.

"But listen to this Shibu-da. I have been researching at the library on this particular topic and have found plenty of solid evidence based upon which we can commission a séance in the Hastings House. Can I show you the reports I have collected from my field research?"

Shibashis turned around and looked at the tall muscular frame of Tapas Dutta keenly. He had known Tapas since many years now as his preferred number two when conducting séances. He strongly believed that if there was anyone in this small team of paranormal researchers who had the skills to become a spirit medium, it was Tapas. "Hmm, I see, but before we see your stuff, can someone remind me where exactly the Hastings House is? I faintly recall that it is in Alipore area."

Someone stood up and shared the details of the location and background information with the group. The Hastings House was a small part of the Belvedere Estate; one of the oldest establishments in Alipore, Kolkata. Warren Hastings had built the Hastings House for himself and then it became the Governor's residence until the Governor House, now known as Raj Bhavan, came up later. The Belvedere Estate also housed the National Library of India, the largest in India, in its sprawling 30-acre campus. It was located near the famous Alipore Zoo in Kolkata.

"Ok, got it now. I think I must have noticed it while driving along the Belvedere Road. Continue Tapas. Share with the team what you have found." Tapas nodded and adjusted his glasses which had slipped down his nose.

"So, there is enough documented evidence that this house is haunted. I will first read out to you this archive dated July 1884 which is a written statement by someone named Paul Bird, a Briton and a resident of Calcutta."

Tapas glanced around the room to check if everyone was attentive and then proceeded.

"One evening, just at dusk, I was returning home from the office in my buggy, with lamps lighted. It was dusk, but in the shadow of the trees overhanging the avenue approaching the Hastings House, it looked pretty dark. I was driving pretty fast, when I heard what appeared to be a run-away coach coming from the Hastings House towards me. I immediately checked my horse and peered

ahead to see how to avoid the approaching danger, but as the noise did not seem to get any nearer, I cautiously proceeded, and when about a hundred yards from house, distinctly saw the reflections of my lamps on the panels of a carriage in front of me, proceeding the same way, that is towards the Hastings House. I kept my eyes on the panels, so as not to run into them. The coach turned to the left to go under the portico, followed by me, but when I arrived there, there was no coach...it had disappeared! I was very much puzzled at this, but should probably have thought nothing more about it, had not my wife, who was watching my arrival from an upper window, asked me at once, "What coach was that just ahead of you?"

Tapas put down the paper he was carrying and looked at Shibashis who seemed to be lost in deep thought. Sensing that the guys were awaiting his reaction, he sat upright and said "Very interesting indeed, but this story does not directly point towards the existence of Warren Hastings's ghost." There were murmurs about how tough it was to convince Shibu-da. Rimli again shot a glance towards Tapas who was now standing facing everyone. Tapas smiled expectedly and instantly fished out another paper. He held it high over his head in a somewhat triumphant manner. "Shibu-da, please listen to this piece of evidence now. This article, which I managed to photocopy with great difficulty, is from the Life magazine issue from the year 1947. May I continue?" Shibashis looked up from his cell phone and nodded. Tapas read out aloud:

"One of the occupants of the mansion in the 20th century was Sir James Taylor and his wife Lady Braid Taylor. Sir James Taylor was the Governor of the Reserve Bank of India from 1936 to 1943. He and his family spent a considerable portion of their Indian sojourn in this mansion. Now Lady Braid Taylor had given her impressions of this historic mansion and the ghostly problems she had to encounter there. She had listed the apparitions, maniacal hyena-like laughter and many other paranormal incidents she experienced in the building. She had heard the coach and horses driving up towards the mansion many times, but never saw them. Even her sceptical husband Sir John Taylor had confessed about hearing the horses. But her most vivid impression of the ghost-ridden mansion was when she returned to the edifice after a sojourn in the UK. In her own words – "My arrival was just before Christmas, with my toddler son. My husband's dressing room had been converted into a night nursery and at midnight of the Boxing Day when the nanny was out, I heard the baby crying. It was something unusual, for he generally slept soundly. When

GRAVEYARD SHIFT

I went to him he was wide awake and much inclined for conversation and I thought if I told him to go to sleep, it would take much longer time than if I listened to him until he would become tired enough to sleep of his own free will. We went on interacting, he in his puerile way and I trying to understand what he was saying. And then he suddenly said in a concerned tone, "Mummy, send that man away!" I thought he was half asleep and was murmuring in a dreamy way, but he went on repeating the same request more forcibly. Not wanting to excite or annoy him, I said: "All right baby, but which man?" He pointed his index finger to the only wardrobe inside the room and said, "That one mummy! The one dressed like a soldier in red and white, with his tail folded back." A few more questions from my side and his answers were sufficient to satisfy me that he was accurately describing a person dressed in the directorial uniform of Warren Hastings's time."

"Very interesting indeed," said Shibashis looking visibly excited. "And now I can very well figure why you guys thought of the Hastings House in the first place – we are approaching New Year's Eve when the spectral manifestations are supposed to be the strongest!" Seeing Shibu-da agog and smiling, everyone in the room began chattering excitedly. Tapas's eyes were already glowing in anticipation of the adventure ahead.

"Alright guys, I agree now that we should investigate the Hastings House. I will let Tapas work out the details of the plan, as always. However, I need to know a couple of things beforehand. First and foremost, how do we enter the house and spend the night there? I do not want to do things stealthily. We all know what a disaster our last expedition to the lighthouse at Diamond Harbour turned out to be. What is the situation here?"

"It is going to be smooth Shibu-da. Rimli has connections with the MLA of Alipore area, and she can arrange us an entry inside the Hastings House for conducting research work. No one will then ask any questions once we have the special entry pass."

"Good and bad," Shibashis said.

"Sorry, I did not understand."

Shibashis got up from his seat and walked a few steps towards the window. He peeped down at the passing noisy traffic of Kolkata and tossed the stub of the cigarette. Then he turned to

Tapas and said, "That means she has to be a part of the circle." Shibashis appeared to be a bit dissatisfied at this proposition. Tapas sensed it would be awkward talking about the circle in front of everyone. He quickly stepped in and suggested he and Shibu-da should talk this out later amongst themselves. "Ok then, let's begin the preparations for spending a night in the Hastings House!"

Later that evening, when Tapas and Shibashis were alone, Tapas took out the topic of Rimli. He could not understand Shibashis's concern.

"You still have a lot to learn my dear friend," Shibashis said. "It is for her personal safety. She is a beginner and will be in grave danger if left alone in some corner of the mansion. The two of us need to protect her from any malicious spirit. Proper shielding and grounding, Tapas, always keep that in mind. He stressed on that once again: "Always keep that in mind. Else do not take her along at all. Is that possible?"

For a moment, Tapas considered what Shibu-da had said and then shook his head. She was their gate pass to the place. "Ok, let's include her in the circle. By the way, how many should form the circle?"

"Five in the circle and the rest stationed at different places covering all major locations of the mansion. You choose the five, essentially you, me, the girl and two others. Take another girl to make it 3 male, 2 female composition instead of a skewed 4 male 1 female compositions."

"Ok, understood. I will get going. I have a lot of work to do."

"Sure. And don't forget to explain everything to that new girl... what's her name...I always keep forgetting!"

"Rimli... Rimli Chatterjee."

"Ah yes, Rimli it is. I will leave it up to you to coach her well."

"Bye."

"Bye for now. Let's get together in a few days to check the preparations."

~~~

GRAVEYARD SHIFT

The team re-grouped two days later for a briefing. Tapas stood behind a table covered with a white cloth. On the table lay several types of ghost hunting instruments, widely used to record paranormal activities. He picked up the first one and said:

"Rimli, do you know what this is? You are new, so I would urge you to pay close attention to what I am going to say."

"Yes sir, sure. No, I do not know what that is."

"This is a FLIR i3 thermal imaging camera. It has a sensitivity of less than 0.15 degrees Celsius. It takes thousands of calibrated temperature readings in every shot. This thing shows any hot or cold spots before you even feel them."

Tapas kept the device down and then picked up another instrument. "And this thing is called a tri-field EMF meter. This will measure even the slightest change in the non-ionizing electromagnetic spectrum. It covers all bases; magnetic, electric and radio /microwaves."

Someone raised a doubt. "How does this EMF meter help us in detecting the presence of ghosts?"

"Good question. The premise at work here is that ghosts must be using some kind of energy to manifest."

Tapas looked at Rimli who nodded her head to show she had understood. "Very well, let us move on now to the next one. Now this instrument here is a digital voice recorder. It's a device to pick up and record the voices from spirits. Sometimes one gets a clear voice, sometimes it seems like a hissing hoarse sound. In my experience, I have heard some convincing sounds which can qualify as concrete evidence but at other times I have also come across crap. One needs a lot of practice and skill to decipher the readings. Amateurs often make a mistake of hearing the slightest sound and then jumping to a conclusion that it is the voice of a spirit."

Tapas paused and answered a few more questions about how to set the meter and take readings. He also shared some insights from his own extensive field investigations. Then he turned to the digital camera and addressed the team lightly.

"And this device requires no introduction. The ubiquitous digital camera. Often just clicking pictures randomly also yields surprising results. The most common thing captured are orbs, they look like little balls of light. I'm not sure myself whether those are just dust particles near the lens or something else, but some people believe those are the first signs of a spirit trying to manifest."

Rimli listened to everything with fascination, diligently scribbling down notes. After the session Tapas asked her about the progress on getting entry into the Hastings House. She informed that by weekend she would be able to secure the necessary permissions, all neatly done with a written approval from the appropriate authority. Tapas was glad to hear the update and later when the group had dispersed called Shibu-da to apprise him. Everything was going as per plan. In a few days New Year's Eve would be knocking at their doorstep.

The group met again just one day prior to the D-Day, this time Shibashis was presiding over the meeting to check on all the preparations. He read through the letter which Rimli had managed to obtain and nodded his head in appreciation. Rimli felt elated at receiving some praise from the formidable Shibashis. Keeping the letter aside carefully, Shibashis turned to Tapas and asked him to present the plan before the group. Tapas stood up facing the team and spoke in his usual confident style:

"I would like to begin by thanking everybody present here for all the hard work they have put in. Let me specifically thank Shibu-da for extending his support and then of course, how can I forget Rimli, without her support we would not have obtained the necessary permission to spend a night in the Hastings House."

I have here with me a printed sheet of paper which everyone will get after the meeting. It basically lays out our detailed plan for tomorrow. I will now read it out. Please feel free to interrupt me if you have any questions or need further clarifications."

Project Title: Investigation to detect paranormal presence at the Hastings House

GRAVEYARD SHIFT

Date: *30 Dec 2013*

Venue: *The Hastings House, Belvedere Road, Alipore, Kolkata*

Reporting Time at the Venue: *9:00 PM*

Team Strength: *10 heads*

Team Members: *Shibashis (Leader), Tapas (Second in Command), Bijoy, Nikhil, Mishti, Rimli, Atanu, Avik, Sudeshna, Emmanuel.*

Members chosen for the Séance circle: *Shibashis (Medium), Tapas, Bijoy, Mishti and Rimli*

Agenda for the séance: *To invoke the spirit of Warren Hastings to appear and answer questions asked through the Ouija board. Terminate the Séance session after one hour irrespective of results.*

Notes: *Emmanuel will be stationed outside the house in the gardens. We will erect a makeshift tent for him and set up all the instruments there. The remaining team members, i.e. Avik, Atanu, Nikhil and Sudeshna will be stationed inside the house at vantage locations to be decided later after we do a recce of the house. The séance will begin sharp at 11:00PM and end positively by midnight. Team should leave the premises before 1:30AM without leaving anything behind. Please be sure to have your cell phones fully charged.*

Tapas paused and looked around the hall. Shibu-da had already reviewed the plan, so there were no questions from him. Emmanuel, who had been tasked with holding the base station, said "What if something goes wrong? What is the plan in that case?"

"Good question, Emmanuel. Thanks for bringing this up. It's very very important, the safety tips for all team members. Actually, Shibu-da would you like to answer this question please?"

"Yes, I better answer this question. So the plan is set and we hope nothing will go wrong. But remember, this is the field of paranormal research and the primary motto here is 'expect the unexpected to happen.' Logistically, I don't think anything can go wrong in this assignment. We have the requisite permission, all necessary equipment etc. Regarding the séance, well, if something untoward happens, we will have to get out of this place as fast as possible; of course, after properly closing the séance session. As I will be the medium, I shall allow the spirit to enter my body in order to communicate with us. If we end up summoning some rogue or mischievous spirit, then comrade Tapas, our second in command, who will be sitting just beside me in the circle, will take over. EVERYONE obeys what I or Tapas says. I hope this is clear," Shibu-da said the last couple of lines with the voice and look of a war hardened army general. His small platoon nodded their heads vigorously. There was no chance of dissent.

Tapas got up and thanked Shibu-da. He unzipped his backpack and took out a black coloured cardboard and a small heart-shaped flat piece of polished wood. "Now begins the all-important refresher talk on the use of the Ouija Board and the planchette. Rimli, Mishti and Bijoy, please pay special attention to this as the three of you will form the séance circle."

"This is an Ouija Board." Tapas held up the board and showed it to the attentive group. "It has a flat wooden surface with the alphabets A to Z printed in two rows in a semi-circular fashion. Below the alphabets are the numerals 0-9. There is a "YES" at the top right hand corner and a "NO" at the left corner. Then at the bottom of the board, we have the "GOOD BYE." There are also a few strange symbols and patterns at the four corners – those are protective spells."

"And this little thing here is called a planchette." Tapas displayed the heart-shaped pointer. "When the spirit takes control, it moves the planchette over the Ouija Board giving answers to the questions we ask. At the start it is best to ask questions which can be answered through either a "YES" or an "NO," and the planchette will slide to indicate that much. As the session progresses, depending upon how the spirit is behaving, one may ask more complex questions like: "In which year did you die?" "Where were you born?" "What is your name?"

"One question sir, how do we know when the planchette will stop sliding?" Bijoy asked.

"You're going to get the feeling that the planchette wants to stop at certain letters. Let that happen and be sure to remember the letters. If you think you may have difficulty remembering, it's perfectly fine to take notes using a pencil and paper. The Ouija board doesn't always use perfect language and may return abbreviated words, phrases and even misspellings. Nonsensical expressions and fragments of a sentence may also point at some meaning when you think about them and view your notepad later."

The session went on for a while, during which, Tapas showed them some video footages of actual séances. Rimli watched with spellbound fascination. She was looking forward to the night tomorrow. It would surely be a night to remember...or forget!

~ ~ ~

The Hastings House lay perfectly silent in the December chilly night. A barn owl's hoot broke the eerie silence, followed by flapping of wings as it swooped down on its prey - probably a scurrying mouse - from its hidden perch amongst one of the massive tamarind trees. The lawns of Belvedere Estate's well-tended gardens hummed with a cacophony of nocturnal insects. Emmanuel sat comfortably in a plastic chair under the bivouac tent which the team had erected, its side-covers flapping with the rising and ebbing wind. The sky was clear and there was no forecast of rain. In front of him, on a table, lay all the four instruments – the EVP meter, the digital camera on a tripod, the thermal imaging camera and the tri-field EMF meter. Just ten minutes ago, the rest of the team had entered the Hastings House, leaving Emmanuel alone but snug in the tent. A ripe fruit fell from a nearby tree into the dry leaf litter making him jump. He looked around nervously and thought, "Would I see the phantom horse drawn carriage tonight?"

Inside the Hastings House, Shibashis was busy setting up the equipment and assigning team members to different locations inside the house. The moment they had stepped inside the house, Tapas had glanced at Shibashis's face. From his past experiences he knew that if there were any spirits around, Shibashis would sense them immediately. Shibashis's normal demeanour had, however, suggested to him that it was not the case. Little did Tapas know what awaited them!

"This room looks perfect for the séance," Shibashis remarked turning to Tapas. "What do you say?"

"Agreed, Shibu-da," Tapas said surveying the room standing with his hands akimbo. "We can set up the circle over there and the camera tripod here."

"Cool. Let us now quickly assign others at their respective positions and get going," Shibashis glanced at this watch. "It is already 10:15 PM. Let us hurry up. I want the séance to start at 11."

Very soon, the team members positioned themselves at their respective points. Sudeshna stood at the entrance door armed with the digital camera. Each member, other than those in the séance group, also carried one such device. Atanu and Avik put up their base in the passageway on the second storey from where they had a good view of most of that floor. Nikhil, being an experienced hand, was mobile and given the freedom to roam around the house.

The remaining five who were to constitute the circle made their way to the room and under the command of their leader, began preparations for the séance. They placed the video camera on a tripod at a place from where the entire room was visible in its frame and atrial recording was done. It was working fine. Shibashis then looked around the room and signalledto Tapas about something. They needed to create the ambience first. They knew that spirits were unlikely to manifest in brightly lit rooms, some darkness was needed to cause their appearance. Tapas took out a mat and placed it in the centre of the room. He put the Ouija board in the centre of the mat and motioned others to sit around the board forming a circle. Next, he took out five candles, five incense sticks, a couple of notepads and pencils. He lit the candles, all of which were of different colours and stuck their bases around the Ouija Board. The flames glowed with uncanny eagerness, as if in anticipation of what was about to transpire. The five incense sticks, all giving out hypnotic frankincense vapours, were placed around the room. A soft, soothing instrumental music was turned on in the background. Finally, the planchette was placed on the Ouija Board.

When all was done, Tapas surveyed the room one last time and then switched off the lights. Curtains were drawn tight and the door was shut. The video camera, already set at the recording mode, was switched on too. The room plunged into an eerie, unsettling, almost portentous darkness. The steady flames from the candles threw menacing long shadows on all the four walls. Tapas looked around at the candle-lit pale yellow faces of Shibashis, Mishti, Bijoy and Rimli. Quietly he took his place beside Shibashis, who looked at his watch. It was time to begin.

At Shibashis's signal, everyone placed their index and middle fingers on the planchette, slowly aiding it to move in circles so as to warm up the board. Shibashis closed his eyes and recited an incantation as a respectful invocation to the dead.

"God our Father, Your power brings us to birth, Your providence guides our lives, and by Your command we return to dust.

Lord, those who die still live in Your presence, their lives change but do not end. I pray in hope for my family, relatives and friends, and for all the dead known to You alone."

Then the chants began. From a dark room in the Hastings House, earnest summons went out in the starry night calling the spirit of Warren Hastings, the first Governor General of British India, dead since 1818.

O honourable Sir Warren Hastings, we bring you gifts from life into death. Be guided by the light of this world and visit upon us.

O honourable Sir Warren Hastings, we bring you gifts from life into death. Be guided by the light of this world and visit upon us.

Shibashis called out first, the others repeated in chorus.

Outside in the garden, Emmanuel was gradually getting bored inside the makeshift tent. It had been over an hour he had been manning the base station. He had seen, heard or noticed nothing unusual. None of the ghost hunting gadgets lying in front of him had recorded anything. He felt an urge to relieve his bladder which was bloated from emptying the entire coke bottle. Checking on the instruments once again, he came out of the tent and headed to the nearby clump of bushes.

Inside the room of the Hastings House, the fervent chanting continued. The circle kept invoking the departed spirit for about twenty minutes, but nothing happened. Tapas felt that the two girls were gradually getting impatient, still they were doing a good job by not displaying any signs of frustration.

O honourable Sir Warren Hastings, we bring you gifts from life into death. Be guided by the light of this world and visit upon us.

O honourable Sir Warren...

Shibashis stopped midway. The candle-flames had begun to flicker wildly causing the shadows to dance ominously. There was a sudden nip in the air. The background music stopped playing and an unnerving silence descended on the room. Tapas quickly checked the thermal camera; the readings had dropped significantly in a matter of seconds. He glanced at Shibashis nervously, who had shut his eyes in deep contemplation. His face muscles were twitching. Tapas knew something was there. He quickly put his finger on his lips gesturing the others to stay perfectly quiet.

Shibashis opened his eyes. He spoke in a soft gentle voice. "Dear Warren Hastings, are you with us?"

Rimli's heart was thumping so loudly that she thought the others would hear it. She looked fearfully at Shibashis as he repeated his question. Then she felt it. The planchette began to slide slowly. It stopped at "YES." A chill ran down her spine. The Hastings House was indeed haunted.

Not all members of the circle were scared though. Shibashis, the medium was expressionless. Tapas felt thrilled – they had succeeded. The other two, having performed séances before, became alert but not afraid.

Shibashis soon managed to tune himself to the energy levels at which the spirit was trying to communicate. From here on, it was a free flowing question and answer session. He asked the spirit a question, and it answered back through the planchette. The video camera placed on the tripod kept recording the proceedings.

"Warren Hastings, do you visit this house often?"

"YES."

"Do you visit this place alone?"

"YES."

"Are you happy that India got independence from British?"

GRAVEYARD SHIFT

"NO."

"How many of my friends are outside this room?

"F.I.V.E."

"What is my name?"

"S.H.I.V.S.H.I.S.H."

"Can you give us some physical evidence that you are actually with us?

The planchette stopped moving. Shibashis instantly regretted asking this question. It was not a good idea at all to ask spirits to manifest in the physical living world. However, sensing the appeared spirit to be friendly, he had braved this transgression.

Outside the mansion, the moon hid behind a few fluffy clouds, and darkness swept the garden momentarily. Emmanuel turned around swiftly without zipping his fly. He had definitely heard a sound. It sounded like some scratching or grating sound. "Could be the night creatures on their hunt," he thought. He hurried in the direction of the tent from where the sound was coming. When he stepped in, his mouth fell agape as his astonished eyes fell on the instrument panels. The readings had gone completely haywire; the pointer arrow on the analog display was oscillating insanely. Meanwhile, the scratching sound continued…

For a moment, Shibashis repented asking that question and glumly looked across at Tapas who returned a surprised stare. Shibashis could sense the energy waves ebbing. The flames of the candles stopped dancing. There descended a deathly silence. For some time nothing happened. Shibashis was about to give up when all of a sudden, the planchette became alive and began to move again. Five excited pair of glowing eyes watched it slowly trace out four alphabets under the light thrown by the flickering candle flames.

"T.R.E.E."

Shibashis instantly felt the spirit's presence as he sensed the energy regroup itself around the room. It was back! Excited, he quickly asked a couple of questions.

"Warren Hastings, are you with us?"

"YES."

"Did you like your stay in India as the Governor General?"

"NO."

And then, unknowingly, Shibashis made the most fatal mistake of the night. He asked that one question which he should have avoided at all cost. Now, things were about to go horribly wrong.

"Were you really guilty of fraud?"

The flames flickered viciously. Instantly, Shibashis realized the spirit had left hurriedly. The Ouija Board vibrated throwing the planchette off balance. And then, something unexpected happened. Shibashis started shivering. His eyes rolled up as the shivers became intense. Before anyone could know what was happening, he shouted menacingly, frothing at the sides of his mouth. But the voice that came out was not his.

"I impeach him in the name of the people of India, whose laws, rights and liberties he has subverted; whose properties he has destroyed; whose country he has laid waste and desolate. I impeach him in the name and by virtue of those eternal laws of justice which he has violated."

Tapas shuddered. He sensed what had happened. But before he could proceed to blow off the candles, Shibashis suddenly left his seat and stood up with a jerk, his entire body quivering. He tilted his head awkwardly to the left almost forming a right angle to his torso and began coughing out blood. At that instant, something pulled the tripod and it came crashing down. Rimli screamed. It was followed by Mishti's terrified cries. Bijoy yelled something and withdrew from the Ouija Board. The guys outside in the Hastings House – Nikhil, Sudeshna, Atanu and Avik – heard the screams and rushed to the room. Suddenly, Shibashis kneeled down and pummelled his right fist on the floor with such a brute force that the bones cracked. Pointing his bleeding broken index finger towards Tapas he growled almost theatrically in a chaste British accent.

"My lords, if you must fall, may you so fall! but, if you stand—

and stand I trust you will—together with the fortune of this ancient monarchy, together with the ancient laws and liberties of this great and illustrious kingdom, may you stand as unimpeached in honour as in power; may you stand, not as a substitute for virtue, but as an ornament of virtue, as a security for virtue; may you stand long, and long stand the terror of tyrants; may you stand the refuge of afflicted nations; may you stand a sacred temple, for the perpetual residence of an inviolable justice!"

Tapas reacted quickly. He was in command now. He ordered everyone to move back as he attempted to close the séance session. He blew off the candles and swiftly rearranged the Ouija Board. He placed the planchette on the board and slowly moved it to GOODBYE. Then he quickly recited the prayer which Shibashis had said at the start of the session. Sitting down calmly, he thanked the spirit.

"O kind spirit, thank you for paying us a visit. I request you to please leave our realm now."

Then he signalled the others to switch on the lights, and draw the curtains aside. Shibashis seemed to have cooled off a bit. Tapas repeated. "O kind spirit, thank you for paying us a visit. I request you to please leave our realm now." Shibashis's body shook violently one last time and then slumped on the ground.

By now, all the team members except Emmanuel had assembled in the room. Tapas ran to Shibashis's prostate figure and called out his name. Shibashis moaned and tried to speak something but passed out. Tapas yelled "Guys, pack up. Nikhil you are in command now, I am going to rush Shibu-da to the hospital."

Just then Emmanuel came running in the house and immediately sensed something had gone terribly wrong. He saw the guys carrying a limp Shibashis. Hurrying over to Tapas, he said: "I have some weird recordings to show to you."

"Not now, we need to get out of this place as fast as possible."

~~~

It was a hot blazing afternoon when Tapas, Nikhil and Emmanuel sat with all the ghost hunting instruments around them, analysing the data collected. This was their first meeting after that night. The shock of the incident had considerably tampered the happiness of conducting an otherwise successful séance. Two days had passed since that eventful night at the Hastings House. Shibashis wore a white Plaster of Paris cast across his multiple fractured arm. His family took him out of Kolkata for recuperation, fully suspecting his ghost hunting avocation to be responsible for this accident. But now, things were getting back to normalcy and the group members had a lot of unanswered questions bursting in their heads. They were intently looking at the screen of the laptop which was replaying the digital camera recording of the séance. After they had finished, Tapas leaned back in his chair and clasped his hands on his face. Nikhil was the first to speak out.

"Tapas, what the hell happened? It was proceeding so well, then why did the spirit suddenly turn so violent!"

Tapas noticed the blinking indicator at the bottom of the laptop screen showing low battery. He got up and connected the external power supply cable. Then he sat down and replied.

"I think it was that question on impeachment which got Warren Hastings agitated."

"Do you think that the spirit of Warren Hastings entered Shibu-da's body and started blabbering those weird words?" Emmanuel asked. He had shared with others his own findings from that night and they were yet to inspect the devices used on that eventful night.

"I wonder," Tapas said while staring blankly at the wall behind Emmanuel. "Actually...hmm, can we have a look at the video recording again?" He gestured to Nikhil who readily nodded and started the video again. "Can you fast forward the clip to the specific moment when Shibu-da asked that question? I want to see the whole event one more time."

After they had finished replaying it, the guys looked inquiringly at Tapas. He was biting his lips and had a thoughtful frown on his forehead. "I think we ended up summoning two spirits instead of just one!"

"What!" cried Nikhil and Emmanuel in unison.

"Yea… basically what happened is this – the question on impeachment no doubt catalysed this debacle. The gentle and co-operative spirit of Warren Hastings was driven away by some angry and possibly malevolent spirit. It was the second spirit which possessed Shibu-da's body."

There was a moment of startled silence.

"But it could well be that we never ended up calling Warren Hastings's ghost at all. It was always some other spirit impersonating as Warren Hastings and it became violent because of that question." Nikhil pointed out.

"Hmm, yes, that could be another possibility."

"But guys, I think we are missing something here. What is the issue with this question Shibu-da asked? If the spirit, whoever it was, either Warren Hastings or an imposter, was so miffed with that particular question then it could have just left without answering. Why did it manifest physically through Shibu-da's body?" Emmanuel said and got up to pull up his trousers which had slipped slightly below his rotund belly.

"And we are also ignoring one crucial thing here. Did you notice that the spirit spoke or rather shouted some strange sentences in a pure British accent? " Nikhil said.

Tapas thought about the points what his friends had raised. He made up his mind and turned to them. "Guys, ok, let's do this. Nikhil, can you sit with the recording and write down the words which the spirit yelled through Shibu-da's body? Next can you please google to determine if we can attribute those to anyone or anywhere. While you do that, let me once more examine Emmanuel's evidences and some other things."

Tapas next turned his attention to Emmanuel's findings while Nikhil got going with the task assigned to him. Emmanuel narrated how he heard some weird scratching noises near the tent and then how all the instrument readings went haywire.

"What time did this happen?" Tapas rubbed his chin thoughtfully.

"Around 11:30 PM," Emmanuel replied tentatively.

"Or in other words, when the séance was on!" Tapas raised his eyebrows and looked at Emmanuel curiously.

"What are you hinting at?"

"I am only suggesting that this matter has confused me completely," Tapas saidwith a sigh of exasperation."Let's go out and sip a cup of tea. I am already getting a slight headache from this mysterious affair."

The two young men stepped out in the hot afternoon. They crossed a busy street and walked up to the tea vendor's shack. Emmanuel ordered two cups while Tapas strode to the beggar sleeping under the archway and dropped a glistening two rupee coin in his bowl. They slurped the simmering tea silently, each one immersed in deep introspection when Tapas's cell rang. It was Nikhil.

"Hey Tapas, come back quickly, I have found something incredible."

Nikhil was impatiently tapping the smooth end of a pencil on the table, his eyes shining with excitement, when Tapas and Emmanuel entered the room hurriedly. Seeing them, Nikhil picked up the laptop and walked up to them. He turned the laptop's screen towards them and announced emphatically:

"Edmund Burke!"

They stared at the html page which Nikhil had opened on the screen:

The World's Famous Orations.
Ireland (1775–1902). 1906.

III. At the Trial of Warren Hastings

Edmund Burke (1729–97)

(1788)

Born in 1729, died in 1797; elected to Parliament in 1766; Privy Councilor in 1782; conducted the impeachment of Warren Hastings in 1787–95, having resigned his seat in Parliament.

Nikhil scrolled down the page as they quietly scanned through the entire text. Tapas let out a low whistle when he saw the lines – exactly verbatim to what Shibu-da had uttered. He pointed out to the paragraph which contained those words -

world, nothing in the range of human imagination, can supply us with a tribunal like this. We commit safely the interests of India and humanity into your hands. Therefore, it is with confidence that, ordered by the Commons,

I impeach Warren Hastings, Esquire, of high crimes and misdemeanors.

I impeach him in the name of the Commons of Great Britain in Parliament assembled, whose parliamentary trust he has betrayed.

I impeach him in the name of all the Commons of Great Britain, whose national character he has dishonored.

I impeach him in the name of the people of India, whose laws, rights and liberties he has subverted; whose properties he has destroyed; whose country he has laid waste and desolate.

I impeach him in the name and by virtue of those eternal laws of justice which he has violated.

I impeach him in the name of human nature itself, which he has cruelly outraged,

"What does this mean?" asked Emmanuel as they sat down around the table. Nikhil had saved the webpage where he had found the speech of Edmund Burke. He shut the laptop and turned to the other two.

"Well, this is my theory. We held the séance and called the spirit of Warren Hastings to appear before us. We do not know whether his spirit did actually respond to our summons or not, but surely, there is no denial of the fact that some spirit responded to our call and did visit us. I am putting my wager on the fact that it was Edmund Burke's spirit who was answering our questions impersonating as Warren Hastings. When Shibu-da broached a topic particularly personal to him – remember the British parliament absolved Warren Hastings of all charges and the impeachment failed – Edmund Burke's spirit got upset. Burke who had invested a large amount of time and energy into the prosecution was frustrated by the ultimate failure of the impeachment. He had warned the House of Lords that it would be to the perpetual infamy of the House if they voted to acquit Hastings. Burke remained convinced of Hastings's guilt until his death. His enraged spirit started repeating the charges it had once famously orated in the Westminster Hall."

Tapas had been quietly listening to Nikhil's elaborate explanation. It did appear to be the most plausible inference they had drawn till now, but somehow he was still not completely convinced. Seeing his sceptical face Emmanuel said "Perhaps you still believe that we ended up calling two spirits instead of one?"

"Yes, Emmanuel. I still stick to my hypothesis that it was definitely Warren Hastings who was with us. Though I agree with Nikhil that after Shibu-da asked that question, it may have been the spirit of Edmund Burke who appeared and possessed Shibu-da's body. But I get this sense that there might be something still hidden from us. Anyway guys, enough for today. I don't think we are getting any further on this matter. Let's keep all the reports ready for Shibu-da's perusal when he returns."

With that, the meeting was over. Emmanuel and Nikhil left leaving Tapas in his room. They had been sitting in his house. Tapas looked at his watch – it was 6 PM. "It's time to go to the gym," he said to himself. He walked over to the cabinet and pulled out a small back pack. Below the bag, there lay a notepad which caught his inadvertent eye. "Isn't that Rimli's notepad, the one in which she was taking notes during the séance?" Tapas picked it up. He looked at the words which she had scribbled down quite legibly and once again his thoughts returned to the happenings of that night.

Q: How many of my friends are outside this room?

A: Five

Q: What is my name?

A: SHIVSHISH

Q: Can you give us physical evidence that you are actually with us?

A: TREE

Tapas frowned. The last question had caught his attention. "TREE? What did the spirit mean by that? I wonder if…" he stopped short and stared again at the word TREE. Something came to his mind in a flash and in his excitement, he forgot the immediate activity which he was about to undertake. Instead, a visibly agog Tapas rushed to his laptop and replayed the video of the séance for the third time that evening. At a certain point in the video, he paused and exclaimed out loud "That has to be it! How did we all miss it earlier?"

A home-bound Emmanuel was riding his bike when the cell phone vibrated inside his jeans pocket. He deftly negotiated the Kolkata traffic and came to a halt by the side of the road. He was surprised to see it was Tapas calling. He felt perplexed, hadn't they just met a few minutes back? He removed his helmet and answered the call. Instantly an excited voice of Tapas boomed into his ears.

"Buddy, we need to go back to the Hastings House. Meet me at 10 AM tomorrow outside the main gate on Belvedere Road."

~~~

The next morning, a slightly bemused looking Emmanuel parked his bike near the front gate of the Hastings House. Belvedere Estate was buzzing with activity. The sprinklers in the garden were shooting jets of water making the green grasses of the well-kept lawn glisten in the warm rays of the morning sun. The gardeners were busy tending to the menacing advances of the unforgiving weeds. Some of the dahlias were in full bloom and had attracted nectar-loving bees. Emmanuel was unsure whether to step inside the compound or wait for Tapas. Just then he heard Tapas's voice from across the road yelling out to him and waving his hands.

"Morning Emmanuel, you do not look too happy."

"Not a bit and how can I be! I had to bunk classes to come here. Can you please tell me what is going on in your head?" Emmanuel replied gruffly.

"Just cool down mate. Come, let us sit on that bench over there," Tapas smiled and led Emanuel to the way inside the sprawling grounds of the Belvedere Estate.

They ambled up to the place where they had set up their tent earlier on that night. As they strolled across the lawns Tapas said "Do you know something about these gardens Emmanuel? Warren Hastings used to love them and spent considerable time and attention towards their upkeep. When he returned to England the gardens of his mansion at Daylesford were laid out after his garden at Alipore."

Tapas looked around and then proceeded to sit on a stone bench under an ornamental shaded arch. After Emmanuel had joined him, he continued, "Friend, we all missed one thing yesterday when you, Nikhil and I were discussing that night's events."

"And what would that be?"

"The spirit of Warren Hastings did give us concrete physical evidence that he was here with us. We just need to find that evidence!" Tapas paused a moment and saw Emmanuel's vacant eyes. He went on,"When Shibu-da had asked his spirit to give us some evidence about his presence with us, the spirit had left us for a while. We all thought it had gone, but it came back and responded by spelling out the alphabets: T R E E. Do you remember that? Now let me tell you that I checked the video recording once again after you guys had left. The digital camera did record the time as well, and indicated that the event occurred sometime around half past eleven. Now, does that ring a bell?"

Emmanuel's gasped as he could read Tapas's train of thoughts "It was Warren Hastings's ghost wandering in the garden which was captured by the instruments!" he exclaimed. Tapas nodded his head in agreement.

"And, my dear friend, look all around us, what do you see?"

"Trees!"

Tapas smiled at Emmanuel whose face was now bloating with a deep pink. He was clearly excited with this new revelation. Tapas continued.

"And, my dear friend, I remember that you told us about your hearing some scratching sounds. What did they sound like, can you describe that again?" Tapas said with a twinkle in his eye.

"Well, it was a strange sound, something like scratching wood with a sharp instrument." Emmanuel jumped to his feet and exclaimed "Oh my gosh, wood! Tree! Don't tell me Warren Hastings left the séance, came out here near the tent, and scratched something on a tree as evidence for you guys."

Tapas grinned, "No better way than to find it yourself, old man. You heard the sounds, now come on, lead us to the tree!"

GRAVEYARD SHIFT

On hearing that Emmanuel excitedly dashed to the exact spot where they had set up the tent. Tapas also got up and strode over briskly.

A squirrel, scurrying on the ground, panicked and darted up the bark of a fig tree just as Emmanuel's feet crunched the dry leaves, littered all over the ground. Emmanuel paused and looked up. He could see the branches swaying gently with the wind. A pair of rose ringed parakeets were making a raucous noise. After some thought, he headed up to a group of large Alstonia trees. Those looked old and were huge – their girth a good meter or so in diameter. He ran his eyes over the trunks and suddenly something on the bark of one of those trees caught his attention. His heart beating fast, he edged closer to examine the bark. He let out a cry of disbelief – there on the bark of that tree were freshly etched a few simple words; words which could not have been carved easily. But Emmanuel knew better, as he delicately traced the roughly hewn bark with his fingers. Tapas came up behind Emmanuel and to his utter amazement, saw the letters which were glowing a faint yellow from the rays of the sun falling in through the leafy canopy overhead.

I WAS H E RE

Just below those words, there was something else. Just two alphabets…

W.H.

A Doll named Wendy

Nilesh was driving his Renault Duster with a cheerful mind. It was a sunny morning. The road was nice and the SUV was doing well. Speedometer read 100 kmph and deep in his heart Nilesh was feeling good for his preference of the car. While negotiating a sharp bend ahead he was a bit distracted by the sudden question from his loving daughter. 'Papa, are we going to see a tiger?" Tara asked expectantly. Nilesh could sense her mood. Few minutes earlier he had said that soon they would be passing though the Sariska Tiger Reserve.

The Gulati family had left Jaipur, where they lived, early in the morning. They were on their way to Alwar and had taken an alternate route this time. Instead of following the usual right turn after Shahpura on the Jaipur-New Delhi highway, this morning Nilesh Gulati felt a bit adventurous, probably invigorated from the prospect of spending a long weekend at his ancestral home. The high spirits had prodded that exploratory instinct and he had headed on to the Agra-Bikaner highway towards Dausa, a small town some 20 kms east of Jaipur. When they reached Dausa, he had veered his car left and headed straight for several miles through barren, uninhabited countryside. They had crossed Sainthal and Tara felt happy to stick her head out of the rear window and let the cool draft of breeze flowing over the Sainthal Dam ruffle her curly hairs. Just as her mother was admonishing her to sit properly and not to peep outside the window, Nilesh had pleasantly declared that the reserve forest was close by.

"I don't think so, dear. There are hardly any tigers left in Sariska." Nilesh replied sadly. "Oh thank god. I was afraid one could jump and snatch Wendy away from me," Tara said clutching her new rag doll dearly. Her parents laughed. Nilesh turned to Vipra and murmured "From where did she find that name Wendy?"

"Papa, you seem to have no clue what young girls watch on television," At this, Vipra nudged her husband, stifling her laugh. "They are inseparable; they eat together, play together, sleep together and even bathe together." Nilesh shook his head smiling and said to his daughter, who was busy humming to herself and was combing the doll's matted brown hair.

"Why do you like Wendy so much?"

"*Arre* papa, can't you see she is so beautiful. I love her big large blue eyes."

"I guess this must be the best birthday present you have ever got."

"Yes." Tara picked Wendy lovingly and kissed her on the cheek. Her parents left the girl to groom her beloved Wendy.

They had covered a good distance by now. Ahead of them, the long road seemed unending and there was sparse traffic at that hour. "Why don't we play some music, some sort of good old country rock? Feel like listening to Country Roads by John Denv…," Vipra was cut short by her husband's panicked cry as he impulsively swerved the steering wheel to the right.

"What the hell, where is he going…," Nilesh never finished his words as the car lost control and rammed head on into the thick trunk of a roadside tree. They were cruising along at well over 100 km/hr. and the sudden impact made one of the back doors to wrench open, throwing Tara on the road. Her head smashed onto the hard surface of the hot tar road. A tragic silence descended all over.

"Why do I feel so light?" Tara muttered as she rolled and slumped on a dirty earth mound in a field full of glowing yellow mustard flowers by the side of the road. The rag doll escaped her clutch. "And what has happened to my hands?" she exclaimed. Her arms, legs and entire body had turned into a diaphanous form. She felt herself and realized she could not grasp her arm or touch her face at all.

From where she was sitting, a muddy path ran crookedly through the ripe mustard fields all the way up to the road where the gnarled and smashed wreckage of the car lay. She could listen to screeching sounds of vehicles stopping on both sides. Men ran towards the wreckage with alarm. They appeared to be shouting and yelling, and one of them first dragged out Nilesh from the crumpled body of the SUV and then Vipra, both unconscious and bleeding profusely. Tara was, however, surprised why the men did not notice her and touch her body which was lying motionless in the middle of the road.

For the next several hours she stuck close to the accident site wandering aimlessly in the mustard fields which were swaying with the tune of the wind. She watched the commotion unfolding on the road. Finally, the wrecked car was towed away and traffic resumed on the road. That's when Tara realized how lonely she was. Tears flowed down her red cheeks. Her parents were not with her. She was alone and something immensely bad had happened to her. A frightened and dejected Tara started roaming the barren countryside desperately seeking the familiar comforting embrace of her mother's arms and the reassuring safety of her father's voice, but she found neither. Soon the air cooled down, birds took to the skies, and shadows grew longer as the scorching afternoon gave way to a pleasant evening. By now Tara was completely exhausted from her futile wanderings. She collapsed under a clump of shady trees near a slimy pond and was about to close her heavy eyelids when a soft and gentle voice startled her.

"Night would be falling soon, little child. Would you like to come with me to a safe place?"

Tara spun her head around and saw the hazy outline of a very old man. The tall figure was strangely emitting a faint blue unearthly glow. He wore pale white robes and had an unusually long grey coloured beard, which was flowing in the direction of the wind. There was something grandfatherly about his affectionate and endearing voice which immediately put Tara's frazzled nerves to ease.

"Who are you? And where are my Mamma Papa?"

The old man smiled and drifted closer to Tara. He sat down beside her and gently patted her cheeks. "Dear child, I will answer all your questions. But this place is not safe for you to stay. Some distance away is located a magnificent fort called Bhangarh where men, women and even children like you live together happily. Come with me, Bhangarh is waiting for you." He paused for a moment and then added "And you can call me whatever you like." the man's smile broadened and lips parted slightly to reveal his sallow upper teeth, while the sagging folds of his cheeks made deep creases on his bluish luminous face. Tara took an instant liking to the old man. "I will call you Grey Beard!" He laughed out loud. Tara slipped her hand into Grey Beard's and they began their long walk to Bhangarh fort.

The quarter moon had momentarily slipped behind the clouds, pushing the countryside into complete darkness, when the apparitions of Tara and Grey Beard finally reached the secure confines of Bhangarh. And thus Bhangarh became Tara's new home after her untimely death. In a few weeks, she was hale and happy again, playing with other dead kids of her age. Listening to the elders, she slowly understood the meaning of death. It was hard for her in the beginning, but gradually she learnt to accept it. But there still was a problem. Tara had begun to miss Wendy terribly; she wanted the doll back. That is when she started visiting Wendy at nights.

~~~

It was exactly two weeks after Tara's tragic death that Vipra first sensed her presence in the house. Nilesh and Vipra had miraculously survived the accident, but their lives had shattered beyond repair. The death of their only child had completely broken them down. Nilesh had taken a long sabbatical from work and Vipra had resigned from her job. By the end of the thirteenth day, after all religious rites lasting the entire mourning period were finished, the relatives and friends visiting them left. The couple now had to mend their abominable existence in each other's vacuous company. Vipra was just about beginning to erase the painful memories from her mind, when Tara returned from the dead. One night, she woke up startled at the sound of scampering feet outside their bedroom. That night she did not pay any attention to the sound, and simply ignored it.

A few nights after the incident of scampering noises Vipra had got up one night to drink a glass of water. Sleepily she walked into the kitchen, opened the fridge-door, pulled out a chilled bottle, twisted the cap open and took few gulps. She was about to return to her bed when she noticed an odd thing – the light in Tara's room was on. Muttering something under her breath, she switched it off, without casting a glance around. Then she went back to her bed. In the morning Nilesh said to her casually, "You forgot to switch off the light in Tara's bedroom. I just did that when I woke up early today."

"What, hey I had to switch it off in the night when I woke to have a drink."

The conversation petered off inconclusively as both claimed switching off the light and they suspected each other, but the fact that the lights were switched on again in the night after she had switched them off did stir Vipra up considerably. It took just one more night for Vipra to confirm her daughter's presence.

That night Vipra thought she heard Tara speaking in her room. A chill ran down her spine as she strained to hear the muffled voice clearly. Vipra got up and decided against waking Nilesh up, lest he admonished her for imagining fanciful thoughts. She tip-toed up to Tara's dark bedroom. By then the voice had stopped. Taking a deep breath, Vipra briskly strode into the room and immediately switched on the lights. There was no one. Puzzled, Vipra heaved a sigh but suddenly noticed Wendy lying on the floor. Vipra was shocked. She had herself placed the doll, subsequently recovered from the site of the accident, inside the *almirah*, along with other items like Tara's school bag, water bottle and some other belongings. These were always kept under lock and key safely away from their eyes, lest those items reminded them of Tara. At that instant all her premises turned into convictions; Tara had returned from the dead.

When Vipra tried speaking to Nilesh, he dismissed it, as she had expected. A proposal to go away from the city was indignantly refused by Vipra, who resolved to make Nilesh see things himself. It did not take long for that.

Day by day, Tara was getting bolder and her spectral manifestations were getting more and more evident. What had begun with just nightly visitations to check on Wendy had now become a matter of all out fun and frolic. From nowhere, she would visit her room, talk and play with Wendy. On one such night, when Tara was caressing Wendy's hair, Vipra peeked into the room and could clearly see her hazy outline. The sight of her daughter's spirit gleefully grooming the doll had reduced Vipra to tears. For some time she continued to watch Tara who was completely oblivious to the watching eyes of her doting mom. Vipra then sneaked back into their bedroom and hastily woke Nilesh up.

"Shh." Vipra cautioned a somewhat irritated Nilesh. "Be absolutely quiet, or she will disappear." She led Nilesh and showed him the incredulous sight. In the faint glow of the night lamp, a stunned Nilesh saw the whitish translucent outline which resembled his little darling, sitting on the floor, her legs crossed and humming a song as she slowly moved her fingers through the doll's hair. The shock was so great for Nilesh that he could not control himself. He let out a yelp in utter astonishment. It made Tara disappear in a jiffy. "Was that ... was that really our Tara?" a rattled Nilesh blabbered. "Yes, it is her. Her spirit wants to play with the one thing dearest to her – the doll," Vipra answered. Now that the scene was all over, the dazed couple slowly paced their way back to the bedroom and retired to sleep, knowing well that Tara would not return again that night. Next morning, when Nilesh woke up he wondered aloud inside his heart whether it was all a dream last night, but when Vipra showed him the new clothes and shiny hair clips on Wendy, he had no further doubts.

They kept it a close secret, not wanting to bring the fact to the knowledge of the superstitious and orthodox relatives and elders of their family lest that might disrupt or impede Tara's nightly visits. In fact, when they thought rationally it made perfect sense to them. In life, the doll was so much dear to her, that even after death her spirit could not let go that obsession. They soon became habituated and somewhat familiar with the spooky happenings and began to accept Wendy's appearances at odd places when morning broke. They knew it was just their daughter's spirit playing with her beloved doll. Some nights, they even watched her secretly, but she always used to disappear if their cover was blown away. Then on one particular night, Tara finally gave them direct evidence of what she wanted.

"What is she doing?" Nilesh whispered into Vipra's ears, as they both stood perfectly still near their bedroom door. Vipra gestured him to be quiet. Tara was sitting on the dining table in the hall with her back towards them and head bent. For a change, Wendy was not on her lap. Tara sat on the table for a full hour or more and then left. Nilesh and Vipra went to bed puzzled at this new behaviour. It became clear to them next morning.

When they woke up the next day, they found on the dining table, Tara's school notebook which lay open. A ball point pen lay open nearby, its cap fitted on the other end. On every line in the notebook, one sentence was written repeatedly; "Wendy please come to me at Bhangarh." It was Tara's handwriting and her parents made no mistake in recognizing it instantly. It did not require any further discussions or deliberations for Nilesh and Vipra to understand Tara's message. It was short, precise and to the point. Nilesh had heard of Bhangarh. That very weekend they drove up to Bhangarh and placed Wendy outside the entrance of that shabby looking uninhabited fort. Sure enough, the nightly hauntings stopped. Vipra was a tad unhappy about losing Tara once again, but Nilesh consoled her that it was the best way to fulfil the desires of Tara's spirit. Several weeks went by, but Tara never visited the house again. Time passed on and eventually they got on with their lives. Wendy and Bhangarh were gradually receding into oblivion until about six months later, on one eventful evening in a busy city hospital, they came across a couple by the name Yamini and Shankar Dikshit.

~~~

Six months after Tara's death

"And of all the beautiful palaces, enchanting lakes, majestic forts and royal splendour that one can find in Rajasthan, I cannot imagine why on earth you want to visit this horrid haunted place." Yamini Dikshit felt cussed. She had to take a day's leave from her business, which she ran from her home, to accommodate for her husband's eccentric holiday idea. An important customer order was scheduled for delivery and this surprise holiday meant Yamini would have to remote control the fulfilment of the same by way of yelling and barking orders over the phone to her incompetent staff.

GRAVEYARD SHIFT

If this was not enough to vex her, there was something else. Shankar had chosen a bizarre location for their day picnic, some haunted fort called Bhangarh, which he said was just 90 km away from Jaipur where they lived. They had left around 10 AM after a rather hurried breakfast and had stopped at Dausa en route to buy some bottles of mineral water. Shankar had conveniently ignored his wife's peeved rants; he knew those would not last very long.

"And what do you expect from the outing and playful activities of an eight-year old girl in a decrepit, abandoned ruin of a forgotten fort? Saloni, your Papa is taking you to see scorpions and spiders and lizards basking their slimy cold-blooded bodies in the hot sun, perched on some ancient stone walls full of welcome cracks and fissures that double up as their cosy homes. Is that your idea of fun, dear?" she turned back expecting some support from her daughter but only saw the blissfully snoring girl, still clutching the comic book in her tiny hands. Yamini sighed and shook her head with exasperation.

"By the way, when we are after all going to this darned place, can you please tell me something about it?" she looked at Shankar and scowled disapprovingly. Shankar seemed to be totally unruffled with her annoyance and coolly exchanged a smile in return. He uncorked the plastic bottle and took few gulps of chilled water. The sun was already high up in the sky and the blazing heat was discomforting. He gave a satisfactory burp which irritated his wife even more.

"And please tell me what sort of phantoms or beasts or unholy critters I should expect to find in this famous haunted place of yours?"

"Ha ha," Shankar gave out a hearty laugh as he gently pressed the accelerator and they sped away. "Let us begin with the description of the place and then we can tackle the point on ghostly hospitality," he quipped. "So here it goes. I looked up the internet and found some interesting myths about this place." his voice now losing all flippancy. "According to one legend, the city of Bhangarh was cursed by Guru Balu Nath. He had sanctioned the construction of the town on the condition that the shadows of the palaces should never touch him, else the city shall be no more. When a descendant prince subsequently raised the height of the palace to such an extent that it did cast a shadow on Balu Nath's forbidden retreat, his curse took effect and the town with its populace ceased to exist. Bhangarh became an abandoned place altogether."

"Mommy, I need water." Saloni said.

"You woke up dear...ok... here ...," Yamini passed her the bottle. Shankar threw a quick glance at Yamini and noticed her anger had dissipated. He knew in spite of her foul mood she had been listening attentively and had got interested in the legend. Saloni drank the water and resumed reading the comic, not in the least interested in the confabulations of her parents. Shankar resumed his monologue.

"Then there exists another myth. This is the tale of the beautiful princess of Bhangarh named Ratnavati. There used to live a *tantrik*, a black magician well versed in the occult, called Singhia, who cherished in his heart a secret love for the princess. One day Singhia saw the princess's maid in the market. He used his black magic on the oil she was purchasing so that when the princess would apply the oil on her body she would fall under his spell and surrender herself to him. The princess, however, foiled his plan by pouring it on the ground. As the oil struck the ground it turned into a boulder, started rolling and crushed Singhia. Dying, the tantrik cursed the palace with the death of all who dwelt in it. The next year there was a bloody battle between Bhangarh and Ajabgarh in which Princess Ratnavati perished with all the residents. Local folklore says the dead men and women inhabit Bhangarh as ghosts."

"Very interesting," Yamini said. She was clearly looking forward to the fort now. She was about to ask something when Shankar cut her "Wow, look at the traffic jam. Wonder what's holding us up?"

Soon they were on their way again. Shankar continued "Back to our story. Bhangarh is the most haunted place in India, partly because of these legends and partly because of media frenzy. There was a reality show on MTV where a couple of young adventurous guys dared to spend a night there. Two movies on Bhangarh have also come out. In fact, I read that Archaeological Society of India has put up a board there strictly prohibiting entry before sunrise and exit after sunset. I hope we don't bump into any ghost or revenant there!"

"Shankar, we are not staying there for long, let me be very clear. We will leave before 3 PM. Do you understand?" Yamini said authoritatively. Her husband shrugged his shoulders and grinned back at her. "Yes Madam, your wish is my command. We will leave well before sunset."

It was noon by the time they reached the place. The sun was blazing in the sky and the firmament around the fort was burning hot. To their surprise, there were many visitors. A big group of noisy and excited college students was swarming the area around the entrance which had a huge 30 ft. high formidable metal gate. "Wow, this is quite a tourist attraction!" Shankar said amusingly. "Come on ladies, let us check the place out. And get your smiles pasted on your lovely faces, as I am going to shoot several snaps."

The fort of Bhangarh set amidst a backdrop of dense forested hills, even in dereliction, managed to evoke a timeless and epochal enchantment which would surely beguile any modern day visitor. The sprawling premises had more than half a dozen temples, large banyan trees and huge untended gardens. Beyond the gardens, there was a water body called *Bowli* in the local dialect. The *Bowli* was a place where sounds echoed in a spiral movement, inexplicably permeating through faraway regions of the ruins. There was also the dancer's *haveli*, surrounded by ruins of many rooms. The entire area was scattered with boulders containing carvings. On a nearby hilltop stood a *chhatri* that was believed to be the past abode of the *tantrik*.

Over the next two hours, Shankar had a great time with his camera. He shot some incredible photos; monkeys squatting on the rampart walls and jostling for a packet of stolen potato chips, a local boy jumping in the *Bowli* pool from a height of about 50ft and a rather scary looking banyan tree. "Coming up to see the *chhatri* of the *tantrik*?"he asked Yamini while wiping the sweat from his face. "Just a quick look and back," he added. Yamini agreed with a statutory reminder "Just a quick look and back to home."

"Mommy I am tired, I don't want to walk anymore," Saloni crashed under the shade of a pillar. "You two go up there, I will wait here."

"Ok dear, you sit here in the shade I will wander around nearby. Papa, off you go now, and make it real quick."

Delighted to be alone, Shankar hurried up in the direction of the minaret. Yamini put down her backpack beside Saloni and stretched herself. She strolled up to a point from where she could see the panoramic view of the surrounding hills. She stood there for a while, glad to feel a gentle breeze caressing her hot face. Saloni sat in silence, panting and puffing, tired with all that purposeless walking in the heat. She was about to close her eyes and rest her head against the pillar when she sighted the doll.

It was lying near the corner of the passage where she was sitting. The doll had large and beautiful blue eyes with three tiny dots under each eye. It wore a bright blue skirt with full sleeves on the hands. A matching cap hid her soft woollen hair, tufts of which fell over her forehead. It was hard to imagine how any young girl would not like such a lovely doll and Saloni was enchanted. She got up. She forgot her tiredness and scampered down the passage. Saloni picked up the doll and smiled. She kissed the doll and clutching it softly ran back to her resting place.

By the time Shankar returned he was genuinely weary. The heat had sapped his muscles and he felt fatigued. Yamini was sitting with Saloni, who was clutching her precious new discovery. "Ok girls, time to head back home. Oh sweetie, what have you got here? A doll! Where did you find it?"

"Over there Papa," Saloni pointed in the direction, "and I am going to take her home."

"But dear, it could be someone else's doll."

"No it was lying there alone. It is no one else's doll. It is mine now. I am taking her home," Saloni replied indignantly.

"Ok ok, cool down baby." He turned to his wife and raised his eyebrows inquiringly which were met with an exasperated just-lets-go-home nod of the head.

"Let's call it a day then. Goodbye Bhangarh. We hope to never see you again, for there is nothing left to see." With that, they left for home.

By four in the afternoon the exhausted family was on their way back to Jaipur. Saloni sat slumped on the back-seat of the car, silently clutching her new-found doll. She had been unusually quiet since they had left Bhangarh. Shankar noticed the lack of usual activity in her, thought it to be the result of her tiredness and called out with a cheerful and engaging voice "So what are you going to call that doll?"

The question made her sit up erect and raise her eyebrows. The thought of naming the doll had not occurred to her. She quickly racked her brains and then in a flash a name came to her mind. She yelled it out.

"Wendy!"

"Wendy? Where did you come up with that? Don't you think a Tina or a Sasha or a Dolly would be a better name?" Shankar got the conversation going sensing it would get Saloni out of her stupor.

"Papa, it would be better if you let young girls alone with their dolls and focus more on things like what you would prepare for dinner tonight. I am not cooking." Yamini interjected.

"Why not order from outside. I am also feeling tired…"

… And the usual husband-wife banter went on. Saloni, on the other hand, kept quiet and sat very still on the back seat. Perhaps she was getting aware of the seething red eyes of a girl sitting beside her and glaring at her angrily.

~~~

"Yamini, be quick and come here. Saloni is running high fever!" Shankar yelled. It was early morning next day and time for getting ready for school. In spite of repeated summons when Saloni refused to get out of bed, Shankar had walked in to pick her up. It was only then that he had noticed her skin was burning.

When they checked her temperature it read 103 F. "She has been keeping quiet throughout the evening yesterday. After her return, she did not even watch her favourite cartoon show nor had her dinner properly," Yamini said worriedly. "Darling, take this syrup it will bring down your fever."

"Wendy." Saloni opened her eyes slowly. Those were red and appeared swollen.

She slowly turned her head to the right, and just inches away from her face, she could see the devilish grinning face of that girl eyeing Wendy, whom Saloni had laid on her bed all through the night. She tried to recollect the dream she had last night. Like an apparition that unknown girl had come to her bedside and was looking at Wendy feverishly. Saloni could faintly remember the chain of incidents thereafter. Finding Wendy in her arms the look of that girl gradually changed from feverish to fiendish and at a certain point of time she even dared snatching Wendy away from her. A distraught Saloni clutched the doll more tightly, closer to her. She asked the girl her name and received her sharp reply in a shrill unearthly voice. "I'm Tara. Wendy is my doll. I know that you had picked it up from the ground of Bhangarh fort". Saloni could also remember what her father had said when he saw the doll in her hand. She was now beginning to perceive what all this meant. She was too determined not to lose Wendy. May be Wendy was in Tara's possession earlier, but it now belonged to her. She had found it lying there abandoned at Bhangarh and Tara was not present there. Saloni had hoped, like all other previous dreams, this one too would end in the morning, but queerly it had not. Tara was not going to leave her.

"Wendy." Saloni moaned in distress, the words hardly coming out. Yamini caressed her hair and placed a wet handkerchief on her forehead. When the sick girl called out the doll's name a third time with particular stress and insistence, Yamini got up to look for the doll. At first, she could not find it, but then she looked on the other side of the bed and found it there lying on its back. She picked up the doll, dusted it a bit and gave it to Saloni, who immediately embraced Wendy tightly, just as she had done last night when Tara had tried to snatch Wendy from her.

GRAVEYARD SHIFT

"Ah," Saloni screamed in agony, as Tara jumped on her and pulled her hair. Saloni only hugged Wendy tighter. She was not going to part with her doll, under any circumstance, even if Tara tortured or harmed her. A distraught Yamini looked at her. She could not make out anything. But she could guess that something like an invisible tussle was going on between Saloni and someone else for the possession of the doll. She could not bear the pain on the face of her child. She asked Shankar to do something and he gave her a sedative dose. The medicine worked and after sometime Saloni began to doze. About ten minutes later she was asleep again. The morning and afternoon passed without any improvement in Saloni's condition, the mercury not budging from 103 F. A worried Shankar finally declared they need to immediately rush her to the hospital. In about an hour's time, they were in front of the physician who was examining Saloni. The distressed couple let out everything about Saloni's present state before him.

"I would advise immediate admission. We need to do a blood test right now," said the doctor. And so Saloni got admitted to the hospital. Even in a semi-conscious state, she refused to part with Wendy, which meant Tara also followed her to the hospital.

For the next two days, Saloni lay on the hospital bed writhing and suffering from very high fever. The doctors were baffled too. Her blood report, urine culture and all other test reports were absolutely normal. From a medical perspective, just by looking at the reports, she was a perfectly hale and healthy child. But in reality, she was far from it. Bottle after bottle of strong antibiotic and paracetamol injections were administered, but the fever did not abate. She could barely speak now, and when she did, the only word which she whispered was "Wendy." It was the second night in the hospital, when she finally managed to utter anything beyond Wendy. She gave direct hint to what was really ailing her.

Yamini was sleeping in the adjacent bed and it was around midnight. The nurse on night duty had just administered a sedative through the intravenous drip and mentioned that she would come again at around 4 AM to check Saloni's temperature. Saloni was sound asleep so Yamini had switched off the lights. The night lamp was on, just in case the nurse came in or Saloni got up. Suddenly

Yamini woke up with a start. She looked at Saloni's bed and was puzzled to see her wide awake and staring vacantly at the ceiling. "What's the matter, sweetie. Why did you wake up?" Saloni turned her face towards Yamini and spoke in a feeble voice. "Mamma the other girl wants Wendy. Her name is Tara Gulati. She will take Wendy away and kill me. Please protect Wendy. Tara is a bad wicked girl and I hate her. Where is Wendy? I can't see her around." While uttering these words Saloni became restless and tried to sit up. Yamini could not make out anything from what she said. She, however, rushed to her side instantly and tried to calm her down. "No more worries, my dear, nothing has happened and see, I'm with you. You had a nightmare dear. It is all due to your fever. It makes all of us to see imaginary things. You will be all right sweetie."

"No I won't be," Saloni shouted with such vehemence that Yamini was taken aback. "Where is my Wendy? I will never let Tara have her. She is only mine. Wendddddddddddddddy," Saloni screamed with all her might.

Yamini instantly fetched the doll and placed it in Saloni's arms. The nurse had also rushed into the room hearing the screams. Saloni clutched Wendy tight, hugged her and turned over her side facing away from the nurse. Even as Yamini was explaining things to the nurse, Saloni fell asleep.

Sensing that everything was under control the nurse left. Yamini was about to switch off the lights again and when she heard a slight grunt. Thinking it was Saloni who had got up again from her nightmares, she turned to look at her, but what she saw totally shocked her. Wendy was not in Saloni's arms. She lay suspended in mid-air! Yamini froze in disbelief and quietly watched the doll move slowly through the air to the other end of the room. Then it lay down gently on the floor. That was when Yamini finally realized there was something strange going on here, much beyond the natural.

Next morning, when she related the events of the night to Shankar, he was unwilling to accept any supernatural explanation behind Saloni's illness. He made Yamini believe it could just have been a dream. Yamini thought over the happenings of the night and somewhat agreed that it did appear farfetched. Perhaps she had imagined it all. Could the constant attendance by the side of her ailing daughter for more than 72 hours have affected her health too? But she was definitely shaken and a nagging worry continued to nest in her mind.

On the fourth night, the things took a turn for the worse. Saloni was urgently wheeled into the ICU. She was having difficulty in breathing. It was only when they began to change her dress when the nurses noticed black coloured imprints of tiny fingers on Saloni's chest. It was where Tara had clamped down her hands all throughout the night. The weight on Saloni's chest had made her respiration slow down. Of course, the medical fraternity did not even remotely contemplate any supernatural cause behind such marks and tried to attribute the markings to some rare form of dermatological condition in which the skin cells die due to unexplained reasons. The condition of Saloni was now really critical. The attending doctor had no other option open before him than to put Saloni on life support ventilation. It was under such grave conditions that fate finally delivered the solution to Saloni's predicament into Yamini and Shankar's hands. It came through a couple by the name Nilesh and Vipra Gulati!

~~~

Six months had rolled by since their only daughter had died in that horrid car accident. Nilesh and Vipra Gulati had somehow reconciled and picked up the scattered shards of their life and learnt to live on. Time had proved to be the greatest healer and with every passing month, gradually the pain numbed, the memories effaced, the past receded and some sense of normalcy returned. Nilesh resumed work and got busy in his office which helped to take his mind away from the horrible happening of the past. Vipra also got herself enrolled for a meditation course. Slowly, the two of them had realized that while they could never forget completely, new experiences could superimpose upon old memories which could be flushed into some obscure corner of one's heart.

"Are you ready? The visiting hours for guests are from 4 to 8 only, so we better hurry," Nilesh said impatiently. They had planned to visit one of Nilesh's friends who had an emergency angioplasty done in the morning and was still not out of danger. Little did they know, in the same hospital, their dead daughter was bent upon taking the life of an innocent girl!

In about an hour they reached the hospital and were directed to the patient's room. While Nilesh sat down and inquired about his friend's condition, Vipra decided to buy some fruits for him. In their haste and hurry, they had forgotten to get something for the patient. She got up and went out in the long passage of the ward which had in patient rooms on either side, glancing casually at each room as she walked past. There was a lot of activity at this hour, nurses running around, medical officers discussing clinical cases wearing white robes with stethoscopes dangling down their necks and visitors anxiously waiting outside rooms. For a brief moment, it reminded her of that fateful day when she had been wheeled in from a blaring ambulance to such a hospital. She brushed aside those past memories and walked on. She was passing one of the rooms near the end of the passage when she glanced inside. The bed was empty but appeared to have been in use as the bed sheet lay crumpled. She kept walking, but then something unusual struck her like a bolt causing her to stop dead in her tracks. While passing by that room she had noticed something lying on the floor! It was something very familiar to her. Completely shocked and holding her hands over her mouth, she took a few faltering steps towards the room's open door to confirm her vision. There was no mistaking, it was indeed the doll, Wendy, lying on the floor!

Vipra soon forgot the purpose for which she had set out for. She immediately ran to the nursing station and made inquiries. They informed her about the poor girl who had been in that room for the last four days, now battling for her life in the ICU. She hastily thanked them, pulled out her phone and rang Nilesh. With a quivering voice she spoke into the phone "Nilesh, we have a serious problem. Tara has returned. Come here quickly."

Ordinarily, the alarm in his wife's voice would have been enough for Nilesh to sit up and show concern. But the shocking message which she had abruptly delivered made Nilesh race out to meet her. When she showed him the rag doll lying in one of the rooms, he walked in gingerly and picked it up. Yes, it was Wendy indeed and no lookalike. They could see the blue coloured stitches on the side of the dress, which Vipra had put when it had torn once. A tense Nilesh carefully placed the doll from where he had picked it up and they quietly walked out of that room. In the passage Nilesh exclaimed, "How did the doll come here?"

"That is one puzzle for sure, but from the nurses I could gather that it belongs to a girl called Saloni Dikshit, who is seriously sick with an undiagnosed illness. They said the only thing the girl blabbers is about the doll and another imaginary girl."

"Young girls and their obsession with dolls," Nilesh grimaced, "I think I know what this undiagnosed illness is all about." He looked grimly into Vipra's worried eyes and met a silent approval.

"We need to save the girl's life."

"And for that, we got to meet and talk it out with her parents first. Hurry, there is no time to lose."

It was an hour later when four tense people sat around a circular table in a corner of the hospital's busy cafeteria. Four cups of coffee, served before them, lay untouched. Sometime earlier, Vipra and Nilesh had managed to meet the Dikshits and ask them out for a discussion concerning a peculiar aspect of their daughter's condition which the doctors had missed. The Dikshits were puzzled initially at such a proposal and showed their unwillingness, but finally the insistence of the Gulatis prevailed. During the persuasion Vipra took the name of Tara, their dead daughter. At once a bell rang in Yamini's mind as she recalled what Saloni had said in the night."Mamma the other girl wants Wendy. Her name is Tara Gulati. She will take Wendy away and kill me." Baffled and a bit afraid, they had agreed to quickly convene in the cafeteria and understand from each other what was going on. Stories were exchanged, each one talking sometimes worriedly, sometimes hysterically and slowly the full picture emerged in front of their eyes. Vipra was shocked at Tara's behaviour. Yamini started to sob, being unable to accept the incredulous truth behind Saloni's strange illness. Shankar held his aching head in his hands while a thoughtful Nilesh went on taking deep agitated puffs from his cigarette ignoring the non-smoking signs on the wall.

"Please save my daughter. I beg you, do something," pleaded Yamini whose sobs gave way to crying now. "Let us just return the doll back to Tara at that fort from where Saloni picked it up," she added. To that Nilesh shook his head ruefully. "It is too late for that, I am afraid. A lot of damage has already happened. Even if we let Tara win this battle by having Wendy, her nefarious spirit won't spare Saloni's life."

"Then what can we do? Should we just burn that darn doll" cried Yamini. At this Shankar comforted her and remarked, "No dear, it will only exacerbate the problem. Tara will be furious and unstoppable. There has to be some other way out of this."

There was a brief moment of silence as each one tried to figure out an answer. Then Shankar spoke determinedly "There is only one way. Listen." They all turned to him as he explained his idea to them.

"Yeah, I agree that is the only option, Come on, we just have to give it a try," Nilesh said nodding his head in agreement. So they split up and got to work.

Vipra took out a piece of paper from her handbag and started writing on it. Nilesh was sitting beside her in the room where Wendy lay on the floor. After Vipra had finished writing, she held up the paper and read it out once, corrected a few words and then handed it over to Nilesh for a proof read. Nilesh nodded and read it aloud.

Dear Tara

You have been a very, very BAD girl. Mamma and Pappa are very angry with you. Saloni is a good girl and now very sick and it is all because of your bad behaviour. If you want Mamma and Pappa to be happy and ready to forgive you, then you should leave Saloni right now. She has wilfully agreed to share Wendy with you. Dear child, the joy of sharing is much bigger than the pleasure of possessing. Discover that joy my child, be her friend, share Wendy with Saloni.

With love,

GRAVEYARD SHIFT

Mamma and Pappa

A drop of tear rolled down Nilesh's eye as he folded the paper. Vipra put a reassuring hand on his shoulder and he gestured to say he was ok. Then they pinned this letter on Wendy's bosom and left the room, quietly closing the door as they walked out. Their part was over. Now they only hoped that the Dikshits would also be able to carry out theirs.

"You may go in now Mrs Dikshit," the nurse spoke softly, "But the stay must not be more than five minutes and don't make her talk much otherwise she'll be stressed." Yamini nodded and the nurse stepped aside to let her inside the ICU. Saloni was still under constant monitoring and doctors had allowed her to be off from the ventilator as the parameters were reasonably stable. She was awake when Yamini walked in. Yamini knew Saloni would sleep off soon as a result of the sedatives she was being administered. Yamini also remembered the advice of the nurse and decided that she must come to the main point fast.

"How are you feeling dear?" she asked in a soothing voice. "You know, I just met Tara outside." At this Saloni looked at her intently. She somehow managed to speak out with a trembling voice, "what did she say Mamma?"

"Well, I scolded her for troubling my little angel." Yamini said lovingly cupping Saloni's cheeks.

Saloni smiled weakly. "This is working," Yamini thought. "She asked me to say sorry to you. She won't trouble you again sweetie, in fact she wants to be your friend. Will you be her friend?"

Saloni nodded.

"Best friends?"

"Yes," Saloni whispered back

"Best friends understand each other. They play together, help each other out. They share their chocolates and even toys. Will you let Tara also play with Wendy?"

There was a brief pause. Saloni looked into the eyes of Yamini who was eagerly awaiting a response. And then came the reply which made Yamini's heart leap with joy.

"Yes."

"That's like my little angel. Ok dear, I will now run and tell Tara. Now you sleep tight. You will be all right soon." A relieved Yamini affectionately kissed her forehead and walked out quietly. She nodded happily to Shankar who had been anxiously waiting outside.

It worked. The miracle happened. By evening Saloni's fever had gone down completely. The doctor explained triumphantly how his team had finally succeeded in saving a child's life. An immensely relieved Shankar stood by the side listening patiently. In another two days, Saloni had recovered completely and was discharged from the hospital.

The plan of convincing the girls to share the doll had finally succeeded. A few days later when the Gulatis met at the Dikshits' house, they were glad to see a fully recovered Saloni running around the house. Going forward, they decided that the best approach would be to let each girl have the doll for one month. They would drop Wendy at Bhangarh at the start of the month and then pick it up when the month was over. Then it would be with Saloni. This would ensure that Tara's spirit never returned to the Dikshit household and remained confined to Bhangarh. Things went on like this for a few months.

There is one last conclusion of this extraordinary tale, something which was bound to happen eventually – Saloni soon lost interest in the doll.

~~~

Nine months later

"Papa can you please buy me that Barbie set I showed you in the mall yesterday, I am so bored of playing with Wendy."

It was a rainy Saturday morning and Shankar was reading the newspaper. They were sitting at the breakfast table. He looked up from his paper at a glum looking Saloni and quickly exchanged glances with Yamini.

"Yes, why not my dear. I guess you are feeling dejected as it's time to return Wendy to Tara," Shankar winked at her.

GRAVEYARD SHIFT

"Actually…," Saloni did not complete her sentence and left it mid-way. She began to fiddle with the fork.

"Actually what dear?" Shankar insisted. He could sense something was in the offing.

"Actually Papa, give Wendy to Tara. I don't want her anymore. Tara can have Wendy all for herself."

Shankar and Yamini could not believe what they had just heard. This was something like the strain of a sweet music entering their ears and they quickly latched on. Shankar agreed to drop Wendy at Bhangarh tomorrow for the last time. Outwardly he showed he was casual and unconcerned but from the inside he was utterly relieved and elated as well. Next day, he drove to Bhangarh for one last time. The rains had made the ruins look magical and mystic, as if rejuvenated with a fresh breath of life. The hills in the background were now covered with a thick carpet of green foliage and even a tiny waterfall, brought to life by the rains, snaked down an escarpment. At the fort, they had figured out a fixed drop and pick up place for Wendy. Every time Shankar came to pick Wendy, he did not have to roam around the ruins. He just had to head straight toward the small minaret of the *tantrik* upon the hillock and there he would find Wendy. So, over time, he began dropping her off also at the same place. He never saw or sensed Tara's spirit though.

"Goodbye Wendy," Shankar said as he placed the doll beside a pillar of the minaret. The view of the countryside from this vantage point was awesome. He took a deep breath of the fresh moist air, and looked around the place one last time. Then he walked away with a relieved heart and never ever returned to Bhangarh again.

Afterword: Although this story is a piece of fiction, the core concept is not! There is a small warning here. Don't ever remove articles or belongings of the dead especially from places, supposedly haunted. The consequences can be disastrous. Stories I write can have happy endings, stories in real life may not!

The Last Wish

Hi,

Good Morning. I want to tell you a story. It is a strange one, something you would have never heard before. It is an epic story of a dead man, who continues to 'live' and will do so even after you and I and our grandchildren are long gone. But before I proceed with my tale, it is quite natural that you would first want to know what is my name, who am I, where do I live and who all are there in my family. Let it be sufficient for you to accept that none of these details bears any relevance to the story I am going to tell you now. But since you still wear that questioning frown on your face, here it goes for your satisfaction.

My name is Prabhat Mitra, a 30-year-old man from Bengal, happily married with two lovely daughters aged 3 and 1. I work with the Archaeological Survey of India in the capacity of an assistant curator. I am posted in Rajasthan looking after the curatorship and upkeep of museums under its fold. A few months ago, I was deputed on government duty to a famous palace, a sizeable portion of which has been turned into a museum and that is where the bizarre events in this story took place.

Frankly speaking, no one around me believes even a single word I have said on this matter. My wife, other family members, colleagues, neighbours and everyone thinks I am making it up. Actually I have none but myself to blame, as I have always been a petty liar cooking up stories every now and then. I just request you to hear me out till the end, and then I shall leave it up to your judgement either to ridicule me or to sympathize. Let's start then, shall we?

There happens to be a singularly beautiful and majestic palace the name of which I am going to withhold purposefully. Located in the state of Rajasthan it has a rather notorious and spooky history of bizarre haunting. Call it a myth, superstition or folklore but the fact remains that local people mince no words about its unearthly reputation. They have heard the legends associated with the palace from their fathers and forefathers, who had heard those from theirs.

GRAVEYARD SHIFT

It was to this particular palace, a part of which the government had recently converted into a museum, I was sent for conducting the annual survey and the related audit work. I was asked to stay for a few days in the palace museum under the gracious hospitality of the Chauhans, who I learnt were the surviving descendants of the last royal family to live in that palace. Perfect hosts they turned out to be, as you would find out in the course of my story.

How I reached the palace, what luggage I carried, which train I took, what time I reached there would be an unnecessarily long prologue so I will only give you a brief account of it.

Prior arrangements were all done by the department and after a short train journey, I alighted at my destination in early afternoon. I found a stately Buick 8 motorcar, quite befitting to the erstwhile regal opulence of the Chauhan royal family, waiting for me outside the railway station gate. I was ushered in that luxurious car and after putting my luggage in the boot the chauffeur headed straight for the palace. The weather was dry, sun was shining bright, though a bit dimmer and the car whizzed past thorny bushes and vast fields along the road. My eyes were glued to the vast expanse of arid land around reminding me of the usual desert areas of Rajasthan and being new to that particular area I was thoroughly enjoying the sight.

I think, this much is enough for you and let us now move directly to my first meeting with the Chauhans. Oh, but before that, let me further take a minute here to describe the palace which charmed me after I reached there. It would be good if you could form a visual image of it right at the beginning of the story.

The palace was extremely beautiful, built sometime in the early 1900, incorporating mixed influences from Rajput, Mughal and European architectural styles. The entire complex, including its sprawling gardens, fountains and gargoyles was designed by an eminent British architect and featured magnificent gothic pillars, elaborate fireplaces, Italian colonnades laced with intricate lattice and filigree work. Its ornate Durbar Hall, which was sometimes the venue of music concerts and other cultural events, had a Venetian mosaic floor, Belgian stained glass windows and walls with intricate mosaic decorations. Ornate crystal chandeliers hung there from the decorated high ceiling. The exterior of the three storey complex was coated with the highest grade red sandstone quarried from nearby mines. The palace was built with all considerations of lavish living of that bygone era - drawing rooms, smoking rooms, guest suites, several grand halls, lounges, cupolas, pavilions, and a spacious dining room which could seat 400 diners at a time. Today, it has three wings; the right wing houses the museum which also has one of the largest private libraries in India. The central wing is closed for public while the left wing is where the Chauhan's private residence was, where I was going to board, as per arrangement made by my office.

On reaching the palace the chauffeur sounded the horn, the sentries in decorative uniform guarding the doorway hurriedly opened the huge gates and the car slowly wheeled inside along the gravelled path and stopped by the side of the portico. Getting down from the car I noticed an elderly gentleman in princely attire standing there to receive me. "Good afternoon," I said bending my head in reverence towards my elderly royal host. I was a bit nervous about meeting him.

"Welcome," Rudra Pratap Singh Chauhan said with discernible warmth in his voice which endeared him to me instantly. "I am informed about your visit and have made complete arrangements for your stay. I firmly hope that you will have no inconveniences here. Now tell me the nature of your assignment and how can we assist in any way?" He said this with such humility that for a moment I forgot he runs a royal blood inside his veins. After I had told him the detailed purpose of my visit and the nature of work, we exchanged some other trivial talks about the weather, travel etc. Rudra Pratap then invited me on a tour of the left wing of the palace. I still remember the strange uneasiness in my heart when I entered that grand, magnificent hall for the very first time. At once I could sense the uncanny presence of someone else inside that hall, watching me.

Perhaps my face gave away my apprehensions, and Rudra Pratap spoke in a light, dismissive voice. "I know you are thinking of all those creepy folk tales you have heard about this palace. Hush, you must not worry at all. It's only him." He pointed to a section of the wall behind two polished marble columns. There were several portraits hanging there on the wall, apparently all of them depicting the life of a man. At that point of time, I was very tired from my travel. The work, I was assigned to do, also needed a start at an earliest. So I did not pursue this topic any further. I asked my host for directions to my room and soon I was lying on my luxurious bed enjoying a much needed late afternoon siesta, thinking about those dreary tales I had heard, but feeling otherwise happy at that moment with all the hospitality I was offered. Little did I know then what lay in store for me!

My room was on the second floor, where a long passage ran around in a complete circle, opening into rooms at regular distance. I think there were eight to ten rooms, I don't remember exactly. The staircase in the centre of the hall opened up into this passage. I discovered later that this passage was the dreariest place in this otherwise wonderful palace. Although, it was embellished with paintings and artefacts, a plush carpeted floor and several marble sculptures bearing ornamental plants, its feel was very gloomy. Even during the day, no sunlight trickled in here and dull, low wattage bulbs glowed desperately to dispel the gloominess, but in vain. To my relief, the room of my host was the one next to mine. The servants had their rooms on the third storey, and no one else stayed on this floor.

Very soon, after getting up from my siesta, I had immersed myself in work, which was mostly concerned with the museum located in the right wing. There is not much to tell about the museum or the details of my work, which was almost a routine one.

By the time I returned to the left wing, it was evening and the Chauhans were busy in chatting with some other local guests in the garden. Dinner was still a few hours away, so I decided to take a closer look at the palace on my own. I was one of the privileged few to be staying in the private quarters of a royal family and was fully bent on enjoying this opportunity. There was that uneasy feeling creeping in my head yet again even though the hall was buzzing with activity, servants cleaning the walls, cooks and helpers scurrying in and out from the kitchen in the far corner. I remembered, this place was supposed to be haunted. As I sauntered along in awe, mesmerized by the carvings and the sheer size of the hall, I came near to that section of the wall which had the portraits of the old man I was shown after my arrival. Curious, I stepped closer to the wall and started observing those portraits with renewed interest.

There were several paintings hung systematically on that wall. At the centre was a full length exquisite portrait done in oil pastel. The man in the painting was bald and wore a flowing white robe. He held a fashionable and befitting mahogany walking stick in his right hand and had a beatific smile on his pleasant face. Behind him was a rocking chair made from a rich variety of teakwood. The rest of the paintings were from his youth. As I was scanning these, my attention arrested on one particular frame. There was something mysterious about it. It depicted the same man, much younger here, wearing strange clothes, standing within the periphery of a strange symbol on the floor with his arms raised and chanting something. He was facing a black swirling mass of thick smoke. I was watching that particular portrait and feeling perplexed, when a hand gently patted my right shoulder, making me jump.

"The weather is so pleasant outside. Can I show you around the estate? I believe the government would like to survey even the exteriors." I turned around, startled, just to see the smiling face of Rudra Pratap. He had noticed me observing the paintings closely. I gathered myself quickly, not wanting to show I was a bit psyched out, and replied in the affirmative. Rudra Pratap paused for a moment, then threw a cursory glance across all the paintings and announced to me, in a voice which showed no signs of fear or anxiety. "This is Mr Chiranjeet Bhagwandas Rathore. He was like my foster father and lived in this palace for several decades until his death a few years ago." Saying this he looked up to the full-length portrait with pride. For some odd reason, I could not share his feeling, and after slipping in a few respectful rejoinders about late Mr Rathore, I gladly stepped out into the beautiful lawns. By then, dusk was long gone and the approaching darkness was somewhat dimmed by the appearance of a crescent moon, the mellow shine of which gave the exterior of the huge palace an eerie look. We had our leisurely stroll around the vast royal estate for over an hour and after that, we came back.

At 8:30 dinner was served. It was a buffet banquet. Besides the inmates of the palace, a few outsiders were also invited. I had a hearty meal and excused myself to the confines of my stately room for a good night's rest. Who knew then that I would have none of that!

My room was like any luxuriously furnished room an opulent palace would have; replete with all amenities and an attached bathroom with a giant sized Turkish bath. No, the room was not a problem at all. In fact, during my entire stay at the palace, my room was the only place where I had enjoyed some peaceful time.

I had dozed off the moment I had hit the bed. The day's travel, my troubled mind after all those stories I had heard, the official work and finally that sumptuous supper had left me with no desire to linger around awake. At around midnight, I woke up suddenly. A strange sound was coming from somewhere outside in the passage. I sat up dazed. The curtains were a little ajar letting in the outside moonlight to streak in. It was a horrible sound, something which I had never heard before and something I cannot describe in words. It sounded like a mix of a growl and whisper. At first, I tried to ignore it, but it was impossible to sleep. I got up to investigate where that noise was coming from. Now, in hindsight, I wish I should have just ignored and stayed shut in my room.

The passageway was almost dark, just a single lamp near the stairway was left switched on for the night. I was careful enough not to make any noises to wake up my host. The sound seemed to be coming from one of the rooms on this floor. That was strange, I thought, as there was no one else staying on this floor. The soft carpeted floor absorbed any sounds which my feet would have made and I slowly walked along the dark passage as it slowly turned upon itself to complete its circular shape. Now the sound was much louder, nearer and appeared to be even more horrifying.

I know it might sound crazy. You would be thinking that this man is kidding. Here he is stalking along dark passageways in a palace which is certified to be haunted. Honestly, today when I think back, I cannot fathom why on earth did I ever step out from my room? Sigh… anyway, let me continue.

Soon, I could locate the room from which that sickening sound was coming. In the dim light, I noticed a hand written message across a wooden plaque pasted on the door – "**No Entry Without Permission**'. The notice was very strange and puzzling as well. I decided to ignore it and head back to my room. Turning around I got the shock of my life. Some distance away from me, in that passageway, stood a figure dressed in flowing white robes, staring hard at me. Oh my god! My heart skipped a few beats and goose bumps all over my body made me shiver to the core. There was no mistaking; it was the ghost of that bald man in the portrait downstairs – Chiranjeet Bhagwandas Rathore. I was petrified with fear and remained firmly rooted to the spot though my legs were trembling, even as the apparition turned around and left. I am sure I did not imagine this, but he just glided away smoothly and could be seen no longer.

I dashed to my room as quickly as I could, locked the door with trembling hands, sought refuge in the bed and pulled the blanket over my head. Of course, I could not sleep that night. I dreamt and had terrifying visions of that bald man stepping out from the portrait and gladly putting me in his place instead. It was one of the most horrible nights, but thankfully it passed without any more ghostly manifestations. And by the way, I forgot to mention, the noise also stopped soon after I had secured myself in my room.

Next morning, I was in a terrible shape and it did not require much effort for my host to understand from my facial expression that the night had not passed peacefully with me. Rudra Pratap was sipping his herbal green tea sitting on the swing in the garden, when he had seen me emerging and moving towards the garden. I had woken up quite late after the night's ordeal. I slumped beside him and blurted out all that had happened. He listened to me intently, but to my surprise did not show any alarm or concern. In fact, I was really annoyed at the words he had uttered, even smiling a little. "It's only him."

I remember looking at him weirdly, which had probably coerced him to take a more explanatory approach. He had put down his tea and remarked. "Son, there is no need to be afraid of Rathoreji. Of course, it was him whom you saw in the passageway last night, but we all see him all the time. As a matter of fact, just before the servant placed my tea here, he was sitting on the same spot where you are now."

That had made me spring to my feet instantly, as if I had stepped on the favourite royal dog's tail. He had laughed out loudly. This was getting stranger and weirder every minute.

"Ok son, honestly speaking, you are yet to know the full story of Rathoreji, hence it's quite natural that you are afraid of his spirit. On the contrary….," he paused and took in a slurping sip, "it is only because of him we can live fearlessly in this palace."

Over the next few hours in that morning, before I left for work in the museum, I was generously fed with stories of 'It's only him' from all corners -- from the gardener to the cook, the maid to the driver. Everyone in this palace seemed to be comfortable sharing their daily living space with a ghost. I was given to understand that he was completely harmless, in fact, his presence was considered benedictory. It was getting increasingly clear to me that I needed to get out of this crazy place as soon as possible. I could now understand why none of my seniors at the office ever ventured into this palace, despite the lure of a lavish stay. It was around 10 AM when I finally headed for the right wing to continue with my assignment.

I can very well imagine that you might have a question about that noise which had woken me in the first place. Actually, the appearance of the apparition had shocked me so much that my senses were numb and I had temporarily forgotten about the noise; you can call it a case of focusing on the lesser of the two evils. All my thoughts and conversations were around the ghost of Rathoreji, the old man. It also escaped my mind then that Rudra Pratap was uncannily silent about the noise. Now that I think back, I feel that I should have taken into account at that moment why nobody except me had got up in the night to investigate into the matter of that obnoxious noise. But before I tell you about that, I must tell what I saw in that closed room. For the rest of my life, I am not going to forget that.

During that day, I got myself occupied with a sense of urgency to complete my work as quickly as I could. By the evening I had made satisfactory progress. While cataloguing the treasures and antiquities, I came across records which indicated that some really expensive and historically important items had been moved out from the museum and shifted to the private wing for safe keeping. The staff of the museum had suggested I could inspect those in the private wing itself since it was not possible to shift those fragile items. The staff duly informed Rudra Pratap that the *Sarkari Babu* wanted to inspect the valuables kept in the private wing. I thanked them, finished some documentation work and then at about 6 PM left for the private wing to complete the last agenda of the day.

I cannot tell how much I was shocked when Rudra Pratap stopped in front of the room which said '**No Entry Without Permission**' and announced to me "This is where the valuables you want to inspect are kept. We call it the Room of Mirrors." He opened it wide for me. I was about to ask him to accompany me inside the room when his wife called from the floor above. He excused himself, and hurried to attend to those summons. I was left standing there all alone inside that room.

Now in regard to the description of this room, well, I can only say that I have never ever seen, heard or imagined any room like this one. There were mirrors stuck to every inch of its expansive walls, floor and even to the ceiling. Ornate, rich and shining mirrors, which made infinite reflections in every direction you turned your eyes. I don't know why but the moment I stepped inside, I felt scared. I could sense hundreds of alter egos of my own self looking back at me accusingly from all directions. The room had at least 10 to 15 artefacts – vases, sculptures, handicrafts etc. which I needed to inspect but my mind somehow would not let me concentrate on the work. I remembered the noise from last night and shivered a little. I decided to have a cursory look at the items and get out of there quickly.

A few minutes passed, I remember I was standing by the giant Chinese porcelain flowerpot churned out in the famous Ming Era. I had just bent down to have a close look at it, when I heard that horrific grinding noise once again. It startled me beyond my wits. I could sense where it was coming from. Slowly and nervously I looked up and saw a terrifying black face glowering at me with its blood shot red eyes. My god, I still go cold when I recall that horrible demoniac face. It was making that noise. Here I don't need to tell you how I felt at that moment, I am sure you can imagine the state of my nerves, but the thing which psyched me out completely was that the face was inside a mirror and wanting to come out!

I remember screaming my lungs out and running madly back into the passageway. I was so frightened that I had dropped my official notebook (which Rudra Pratap helped me to recover later) and had darted out shouting maniacally. I must have made quite a scene, as several people, including my hosts, left whatever errand they were doing and assembled quickly. They managed to soothe me and got me settled in a comfortable sofa. When I told them all what I had seen and heard, there were murmurs and a few shake of the heads all around, more like 'So what, we can't do anything about it'. It was only when I announced to Rudra Pratap my intention to pack up and leave, that he dispelled the gathering of amused onlookers and explained to me what was this business all about and why I should not feel scared!

That conversation, I remember, had sounded more like a consoling father talking lovingly to his young toddler. As I have told you, my hosts were incredibly good and graceful people and the way Rudra Pratap Chauhan talked to me that evening somehow soothed my rattled mind. I will now tell you the story he narrated to me.

"It is important for us that the government takes stock of all our treasures and valuables accurately," he had said to me. "Please don't leave without finishing your task, no official from the government department has ever come to this palace and we never get the grants for maintenance which such a historic palace rightfully deserves." He looked forlorn, sad and by then I had cooled down a little. On seeing me relaxed, he first gave me a detailed account of the palace's history which unfortunately had been twisted and gnarled out of context by the locals to feed their gossip-hungry appetite.

MANISH MAHAJAN

The story went that the palace had been cursed just a decade after it was constructed; a case of obnoxious black magic. No one today remembers or knows the exact circumstances prevailing at that time, but it did happen so that a particularly evil and malicious spirit somehow took its shelter in the left wing of the palace. That is when the stories of haunting began. Mysterious deaths occurred, staff began to fall sick one by one and left their jobs, trees and shrubs began to wilt, birds and bees flew away to a safer place and finally the once prodigious palace became almost abandoned, left to the complete authority and whim of that evil which had consumed it. The royal family tried every known method to exorcise that spirit but all such efforts proved to be of no avail. Priests, *tantriks*, *babas*, *fakirs* from all over the country came but failed, some even vowing never to set foot in the palace again. They were of the same opinion and all said one thing – this was not any ordinary evil spirit! It was the incarnation of some primordial evil, the *Shaitaan* himself. And then someone told the royal family about this young renowned medium by the name Chiranjeet Bhagwandas Rathore. An emissary was sent with an urgent request from the royalty to help them with this exorcism. Chiranjeet took a lot of time to accept that royal invitation. He was only a medium – a person who could communicate with spirits sense their presence, but had no prior experience in driving them out, let alone a nefarious one which had thwarted off repeated attempts by experts of this dark field. When the royal summons grew persistent, with offers to make him a permanent resident of the palace, he finally acceded.

This young man did not possess anything different from the others who came and left dejected before him. They were all exceptionally brave men drawn from all religious faiths, some even having successfully orchestrated difficult exorcisms. However, there was one quality in which Chiranjeet was different – he loved to experiment and he was tenacious as well. While the wizened old men visiting the palace prior to him came prepared with their elaborate rituals and innumerable ghost busting paraphernalia, Chiranjeet had boldly walked into the palace with little or no accompaniments. He had already figured out that this evil spirit could not be driven away by the usual tried and tested methods in the form of incantations from holy text, beating with the broomstick and sprinkling of holy water and mustard seeds as were practiced by the black magicians, *fakirs* and *tantriks*. He had to find some unconventional way – probably fraught with immense risks.

What I have told you is a very abridged version. Rudra Pratap had gone on for one long hour just narrating this fantastic tale to me. The narration in his sonorous voice had transported me back to those times and sitting there in that palace, I could imagine the scenes in my mind and clearly visualize those happenings. If you could have seen him speak, you would have known how he felt about the whole business. It meant a lot to him and especially Chiranjeet Rathore was almost a demigod to him. Listening to his passionate rendition that warm evening, I had but completely forgotten my fears. In fact, I was so engrossed that I had even chipped in with a few clarifications and questions of my own.

"Which year did those events take place?" I had asked.

"Sometime in the 1930's definitely before me or any of my brothers were born."

"And how old would Rathore ji be when this happened?"

"Probably in his early twenties."

There was a polite knock on the door and a servant popped his head in to remind us that dinner was ready. Rudra Pratap would have gone on with that tale had this intermission not made him stop. Getting up, he had said to me: "Rathore ji lived a long life in this palace. He did succeed in getting this place rid of that notorious evil spirit and during the ensuing years, this seat of my forefathers was yet again restored to its rightful glory and fame. He died some years back at the ripe age of 89. His spirit still stays here with us, that is the truth, but I hope you will understand now that it will never harm you."

I admit here that on being given that assurance I had nodded my head mechanically. "Even if we have a fatherly ghost levitating around this palace looking after the wellbeing of its residents, I don't find it reassuring," I had muttered suppressing my breath. It all seemed like a fantastic fable straight out of a children's book.

While some part of me had seemingly relaxed, there were still the disquieting questions in my mind about that horrific black face which had stared at me… and the equally oppressive noises it made. But I held back broaching the topic again, certainly not at the dinner table, where I could see that they had made special dishes just to appease me. I ate heartily knowing well that this would be the last time I was having dinner in that palace as I had made up my mind to depart positively by noon on the next day. Forget the next day, I did not even stay the full night!

After dinner, there was a small recreational event by some local folk dancers and then we all retired to our respective rooms at around 10 PM. I had made up my mind to stuff some cotton buds in my ears in order to insulate myself from those horrid noises. Before going to bed, I, however, decided to pack up my stuff. In my heart, I was glad about my decision of leaving. I had just opened my suitcase and dumped in a few clothes, when I heard footsteps in the passageway. Despite the conciliatory lecture of the evening, I got instantly frightened, more so when the footsteps stopped in front of the closed door of my room. And then there was a knock. My heart would have certainly stopped beating, if a familiar voice had not called out my name. It was Rudra Pratap outside. I heaved a sigh of relief and let him in. He saw what I was doing.

"So you have finally decided to leave!"

"Not now, tomorrow morning," I said firmly. There was a touch of rudeness in my repartee which did not go unnoticed.

"I presume, you're yet to finish your work."

"Does not matter. I cannot stay here any longer." I impatiently dumped another pair of trousers into the suitcase and zipped it shut.

Just then the noise began. Rudra Pratap instantly looked at my grimaced pale face, and I think by then he could well perceive that I would not change my mind. He quietly walked up to the window and stood there resting one arm on the wall, blankly staring into the dim darkness of the palace grounds that stretched in front. The overhead lamp threw light on his white hair which made it shine golden yellow. He turned to me and said with sudden exasperation, his voice rising a little.

"Ok, leave. Go away without even bothering to know what happened next."

I must say I was taken aback by this unexpected outburst. It dawned on me that I was talking to a member of the royal family, someone of my grandfather's age, and I needed to be at least polite and respectful. After all, he and his palace coterie had been excellent hosts, stood by my side on all occasions and many times even going out of the way in the name of hospitality.

"What do you mean sir?" I said calmly.

"How Rathore ji overcame that evil spirit? Why does he wander about this palace even after death? Why do we have so many mirrors in that room? Why is that face in the mirror unusually dark? But no, the answers seem to be unwanted. A young man like you just turns his back and walks away only because he could hear some sound and visualize something unusual."

I remember he had blurted all these out in one breath, his face getting redder with each delivery and squirming with exasperation. I must confess to you I was shocked at his outburst. Not only was his sneering reaction disconcerting to me but equally relevant were the questions he had raised which roused insatiable curiosity in my mind. I simply had to retract from my earlier stand, after all, my job could be at stake if he complained about my leaving without finishing the assignment! One more thing. Inside my heart, I nurtured a sincere longing for having the answers to all those riddles from him.

"Ok sir, please tell me the entire story. I want to know happened next." There was definitely an element of truth in that, as his outbursts had aroused my curiosity.

"No story-telling this time. Rather, I will show you what did finally happen. Once you see it with your own eyes, there would be no need for any questions or answers." I could sense that he had still not calmed down.

His remark had puzzled me. What did he mean "I will show you what happened." I was about to ask him when he had a look at his watch and remarked "It is 10:30 PM now, there is a train which comes at 11:55 PM. I will ask our chauffeur to drop you at the station and make arrangements for your train booking as my special guest. You must leave immediately after you witness it."

I was quite taken aback with the sudden change in his mood. I could apprehend that inside his heart he was still seething and his hidden anger was thus exposed through his words. Somewhere I could notice the usual trait of his royal lineage, graceful when calm but authoritative when angry. I was speechless and had no defence to seek for his clemency. I tried citing pending inspection work in the museum but that hollow entreaty was shot aside sarcastically with a-'you-said-it-does-not-matter' rebuttal. I had been asked to leave. I always wanted to, but not in this unwelcome way.

"Follow me." Rudra Pratap was already walking even as I sized up the hole I had dug into. I nervously followed him out into the hallway. My heart froze when he stopped in front of the room with mirrors, opened the lock and pushed the doors wide open. I hesitated, every inch of me screaming and warning not to enter that room. He sensed my nervousness and came up to me, placed his assuring hand on my shoulder and said in a calm, soft but firm voice, "Fear not, I'm with you." His anger had now gone and he was back to his usual genial self.

"Son, trust me, no harm will befall you. I know you are frightened, even I was so, when Rathoreji himself had forced me into this room and showed me what you are going to witness now." He gently led me in and closed the door shut. "You will now see something which is beyond your imagination and ken. Even if you go back and tell someone, no one will ever believe you."

Although I was thankful for the fact that his anger had ebbed, the thought of me being witness to something paranormal made me really uncomfortable, a feeling which I tried best not to show on my sweaty face. I was not afraid for my life or of any physical harm, in that I trusted Rudra Pratap's confident assurances; what unnerved me the most was that I had to complete what had begun, against my will. I did not want to hear, listen, know or see the epic story of the old bald man slaying that evil spirit, the beast. I did not really care about those unsettling mirrors and their thousand reflections. I just wanted to run away from that room, that floor, that palace and that city to the cosy and safe association of my wife and daughters. But I could not.

Rudra Pratap fumbled for a moment in the darkness searching for the power switch board, and then switched on all the lights. Instantly a thousand reflections sprang to life, some looking at me sneeringly, and some sympathetically. By the way, there was no noise now. It had stopped.

I was completely shocked by Rudra Pratap's next statement. He had taken a few steps forward and was standing beside that Chinese porcelain flowerpot. He pointed to a mirror and said "Come, we need to enter that mirror." It was the same mirror where I had seen that terrifying black face making those grotesque noises.

I think Rudra Pratap understood that my reservoirs of strength and sanity were fast depleting and he did not waste much time waiting for my reactions. He had quickly added "Ok son, listen to me carefully and I request you to throw out from your mind reason, logic, rationale and science for a moment; because looking through the lens of those viewpoints, nothing would make sense to you. The world beyond our living realm cannot be construed by logic or rationale. This mirror here is the entry gateway to that other world and that one over there...." He sprang around and pointed to another mirror near the door. "That one is the exit. We need to step into this and we will step out from that. To hide these two gateways to the spirit world, we had to camouflage this whole room with numerous identical mirrors so no one could find the real ones easily. We did not want any unsuspecting individual to accidentally drop into the other world and never come out. Two servants went to clean that mirror and were never seen again," he said sadly.

How I wish I could see the expression on your face! Unbelievable isn't it? Just imagine how I would have reacted to all this! I was petrified. I think Rudra Pratap knew I would never be convinced to do this alone, hence he had consciously used the 'we' while saying "come, we need to enter that mirror." But he had overestimated my courage as I did not budge an inch from my place. It was he, who then volunteered to go alone first and show to me it was totally safe. Before I could have reacted, he confidently strode up to the mirror and coolly walked into it!

When he disappeared, it struck me that I was now alone in that ghastly room. I had wondered which was better, being alone in the room or being with him inside that mirror. Somehow I trusted the man for his words and his absence made me really scared. I was wondering should I just turn around and run away that very moment, when to my utter disbelief and astonishment Rudra Pratap suddenly stepped out from the mirror he had called out as the exit. He had been away only for a few seconds. He walked up to me and said.

"Look at me, standing before you, all hale and healthy! It is not harmful at all."

I said nothing.

"It is 10:50PM already. Let us make a move now young man. You have a night train to catch."

And thus, however incredulous this may sound, we both stepped into the mirror. We entered the other world and came out of it just five seconds later. But hold on, there is a subtle twist. I meant five seconds of the living world, the spirit world's time scale is totally different. Roughly, 1 sec of our life equals 1 hour there, which means Rudra Pratap and I were inside the mirrors for a full 5 hours. Yes, 5 hours, during which I was shown 'what happened next'. 5 hours in which I found the answers to all the questions. 5 hours, that will remain etched forever on my mind. Now, I am not going to describe the happenings during those full 5 hours in detail. Although I would appear to be rushing through the story, please be aware, all that I am going to tell you now transpired slowly and gradually. So my friend, listen to what happened to me in those 5 seconds or 5 hours, whichever way you choose to look at it.

After stepping into the mirror, I found myself standing in the garden of the palace's private wing. But lo! This was an unkempt garden, full of rotten leaves, littered all around. The garden was devoid of any grass cover, with wild shrubs having eaten up the rightful places of roses, dahlias and marigolds. The line of tall eucalyptus trees along the path to the palace were denuded of any leafy cover and their dry, sagging branches had no place for the frolicking mynahs or pigeons. The sun was overhead, shining brightly on the palace walls which were covered with thick moss and cobwebs. The paint and plaster had worn off at several points, revealing the unevenly laid stone blocks underneath. It was indeed pitiable to look at this decrepit property, apparently lying abandoned since years. I blinked and pinched myself, but it was real, I had moved back in time!

From the door a young man came out, whom I instantly recognized as Mr Chiranjeet Bhagwandas Rathore, the medium. He was walking towards us with a beatific smile on his radiant face. He came closer and closer till he was an arm's length away from my face, but still he did not stop. In the next moment, he was about to crash into me. I let out a low cry and raised my hands, but he just walked into me. Before I knew what was happening, he and I (we were one body now) merged into Rudra Pratap! Then I understood. Rudra Pratap and I were inside his body which meant we would see, hear, sense and feel everything which he would. That was what Rudra Pratap had meant about showing me instead of telling me what happened next. That was why he had asked me to step into the mirror.

So, for the rest of the narrative please keep in mind that while I refer to Chiranjeet from a third person perspective, it is actually me who is seeing and experiencing everything. Fantastic, isn't it! Ok, back to the story.

Chiranjeet stood in the hall looking around nervously. He could sense something already, but this something was unlike any entity he had encountered before. Being a practicing medium, he had often interacted with spirits of dead people, sometimes even going as far as letting a friendly one enter his body. In this palace, the feeling of negativity was so intense that for a moment he felt a blinding and excruciating pain in his head. He realized that this exorcism would have to be done deftly but also quickly, or else he would be putting his own life in grave danger. He immediately sat down in a cross-legged position, closed his eyes, controlled and slowed down his breath and chanted a few ritualistic verses. He was summoning that deadly evil spirit.

Something shook underneath. There came a rumbling sound from one of the palace's several underground cellars, which was followed by that intense shaking. The wind picked up outside and a few dry leaves from the garden flew inside the hall. And then there was that all too familiar horrible grating noise, the location of which was distant at first but as it slowly grew louder and louder, it could be felt that the source was constantly changing its position. It was rapidly closing in. The very next instant a pall of thick, black smoke madly hissing ushered into the hall from one of the rooms. It then headed straight for Chiranjeet. I remembered the painting on the wall and it now made sense to me. Suddenly Chiranjeet's concentration broke and he was totally enveloped in a dark black coloured mist. Sooty air entered his thorax, reached his lungs and a burning sensation made him cough and wheeze in extreme pain. The supernatural vile entity had made its intention very clear.

Chiranjeet ran out of the hall, dashed up to the stairway trying to get away from that thick black smoke. The passageway on the second floor was dark and he blindly ran into one of its rooms. He quickly locked himself in and waited. I shuddered when I realized that this was the very same room – the room of mirrors! He was panting heavily. He looked around the room and saw two beautiful mirrors covered in a veneer of thick dust. He put up his hands over his nose, there was a putrefying stench coming out from somewhere. He soon traced where it was coming from; a dead human corpse, probably one of the priests who had unsuccessfully tried to accomplish what he himself was trying to achieve. Looking at the cadaver, lying at the farthest corner of the room, a sudden flash of thought occurred to him. "This evil entity in its fluid smoky state is quite impossible to tackle. It is just too powerful. I must at least reduce it to a state equal to mine if I am to have any chance of fighting and overcoming it." And he set up a ploy to trap the entity in the tangible confines of that cadaver.

This time around, he purposely opened the door and summoned the spirit with increased vigour, challenging it, even mocking it. When it came rushing at Chiranjeet like a full-charged steam engine, panting and hissing with unending fury, he quickly uttered the magic chants. This time the spell worked! The swirling black smoke stopped spreading further, got sucked into the corpse which immediately came to life and sprang to its feet. Its complexion also changed from fair to pitch black and with horror I saw the same face which had stared at me from the mirror. The spirit realized it was now entrapped in a physically degradable body from which it was unable to escape due to the spell. Chiranjeet had won round one of the battle. It became evident that the adversary could be defeated.

Enraged, the corpse let out a shrill, spine-chilling scream and savagely lunged at Chiranjeet, but could not touch him. Chiranjeet had drawn some strange symbols along a circle on the floor. This created a protective sheath like an air capsule. He was safe as long as he remained inside that circle. But he knew that the spell would not last long. If the spirit needed to be driven away, he had to think something more effective. And the action must be initiated fast. The symbols would start to disappear in a few hours and then the corpse would tear him apart limb by limb, tendon by tendon.

"You don't have a chance. I order you to leave this palace now." Chiranjeet hollered at the corpse. He knew the spirit would talk back to him as now it had a host body.

"Ha ha ha," the corpse broke into a deeply unsettling and evil laugh. "That's what everyone before you had said too. Look what I did to this one," he replied in a sneering voice which belonged to neither a man nor a woman. It was the queer voice of an evil spirit, something no human would have ever heard.

"You think you are very smart." Chiranjeet was now trying to deceive the corpse into committing a mistake. There was no way he could have exorcised this unearthly 'creature'. Mere exorcism was not the solution. The only way out was to trap the spirit and get it confined securely and permanently.

The supernatural duel went on for a couple of gruelling hours but none could overpower or outwit the other. Sometimes frustrated, the corpse would walk out of the room and start wandering in the passageway, his dreadful voice echoing throughout the floor, reverberating inside the whole palace. Chiranjeet, of course, could not move beyond his limited periphery of protection; he would just sit down there and meditate, frantically focusing on his faculties for a new stratagem. The strength of that protective circle was getting weaker and weaker by every passing minute, only a few inches of the invisible protective wall separated him from certain death. It was in this desperate situation that Chiranjeet's eyes fell on the mirror and an innovative idea struck him. That was it! He had to grab that last chance or else get eaten raw by that evil spirit.

He called out to the living corpse, who was now crawling on the floor, sniffing the air with his half rotten nose. "How about a game to end this once and for all?"

"What sort of a game?" the corpse looked at him sharply.

"A game of chance. Rolling of the die. If I win, you will have to walk into that mirror and never step out. In case of your win, of course I won't live to see what you will be doing next." Saying this, Chiranjeet let a die drop to the floor from his outstretched palm. It rolled to a stop near the corpse's hairy feet.

The corpse let out a menacing laugh. "Nice. I like you. You are different. Ok, let's play but on one particular condition. If I lose, I still get a chance of expressing my last wish and at any cost that has to be fulfilled."

"As long as you vow to stay confined inside the mirror till the end of time, I am going to grant whatever last wish you may have."

"Ah, how confident you sound! Let the die roll. Each one of us gets the chance to throw the die three times. The one with the lowest score will be the loser."

"Agreed, you go first. Rules are set, let the game begin."

The corpse took the first draw. It was a four. When Chiranjeet tossed it, it rolled to stop at two. There was a rapturous shriek from the corpse. Round 1 had gone to him with a 2 point lead. For the next set of throws, they changed the order in between. Chiranjeet went first and then the corpse.

The die rolled on a bit farther, bumped against the leg of a chair and stopped. The chair obstructed Chiranjeet's view. The corpse leapt to check the score. It was a six! He was enraged, and with his back completely blocking Chiranjeet's view, he gently tipped the die over one face so that the top now showed three dots. Grinning smugly, he called out "It is a three," and picked it up to show Chiranjeet, whose face now became grim and sweaty. Would it end like this? His fear finally turned into absolute terror when the corpse's next throw yielded a four! Round 2 had again gone to the corpse, who moved ahead with an overall lead of 3 points. Chiranjeet's heart sank. The corpse was thumping his hairy chest and licking his thick black lips in anticipation of a sumptuous meal. There was a menacing yet gleeful glint in his eyes. Victory was near. Just two more throws of die were left now. In fact, if the corpse could strike at least a four or a five or a six, the maximum, there would not arise any need for the last throw.

He quickly grabbed the die, cupped his hands and shook them, the die rattling inside. He did cast his vicious look at Chiranjeet and joyfully exclaimed with a certainty, "Here it goes. You are doomed." Then he threw the die. It bounced around and stopped near Chiranjeet's feet this time. It was a two!

Chiranjeet closed his eyes and thanked the heavens. He was still in the fray with a final chance. One last throw of the die would end this horrid and uncertain game. He looked upwards, muttered a silent prayer and picked up the die. The corpse had been edgy as well. He was impatiently waiting for the last throw to happen. With a deep breath, eyes still shut, an expectant and desperate Chiranjeet let the die roll out slowly from the palm of his outstretched hand. Time froze for a few seconds when the die rolled on the floor reluctantly, losing its spin. And then it came to a stop. It was a six, the maximum. The beast in utter despair screamed out so loud that it must have torn a few ligaments inside his throat. Then it started moaning and wailing, smashing and thrashing everything which came in its way. Chiranjeet had finally won.

The next thing I remember was falling out from the exit mirror with a severe jolt. It happened so suddenly and with such severity that for a moment, there was an unbearable stinging pain all over my body, as if something was forcefully removed from me. But it ebbed gradually and there I lay, completely speechless and stunned.

The ever caring Rudra Pratap was kneeling beside me, anxious yet smiling. I looked at my wristwatch; it was still 10:50 PM. "Son, it is over. Come, I will drop you to the waiting car."

I walked down to the hall led by Rudra Pratap, he had insisted on my sipping a strong cup of coffee. He sent for a boy to haul my luggage down and stow it in the boot of the royal car. I had not uttered a single word since coming out of the mirror.

"So, looking forward to the trip back home?" he asked me gently.

I said nothing. I was too dazed to get into any rhetoric.

"I trust you will now appreciate, understand and respect what Chiranjeet Bhagwandas Rathore did. That is all I wanted you to know."

I took some sips of the brew from the steaming cup, it felt nourishing and the warmth freshened me. I nodded my sincere yes.

It was time to leave. To tell you frankly, at that moment I had mixed feelings. It was true that I wanted to get out of this dreary place, but after knowing the full truth, the place had endeared itself to me. I could now perceive that apart from Rudra Pratap, the royal descendant, I was the sole fortunate man before whom a great mystery was revealed. Before leaving the palace I paused in the hall where the large paintings hung. For one last time, I looked at those, this time with a mingled feeling of awe and reverence and once again I shuddered and felt goose bumps all over my body, maybe for the last time. The paintings made perfect sense to me now. And then, I remembered something and turned to Rudra Pratap.

"Sir, what was the devil's last wish?"

Rudra Pratap let out a deep sigh. "Even in his defeat, the wily critter salvaged some victory with that last wish of his. He asked Rathoreji to never step out of this palace."

I considered this for a while and then remarked, "I see, that's why he spent his entire life in this palace."

"Did I not tell you, never ever. Rathoreji was not allowed to leave the palace even after his mortal death."

I fell silent. I could well imagine that Chiranjeet Bhagwandas

GRAVEYARD SHIFT

Rathore's benevolent spirit would ever continue to roam the halls and rooms and passageways of this majestic palace till the end of time. The devil's last wish had bound him to it, forever. At the doorway I had to pause one more time, for a few seconds only as I could hear a different sound. I turned back only to see the chair near the table below the stairway rocking on its own. Just for a brief moment, I saw a white hazy human form sitting on it. Probably Rathoreji also was saying his goodbye to me. I became pensive and smiled. Then I stepped out into the night.

This, my friend, was my incredible story. It is the epic story of a dead man, who continues to 'live' and will do so even after you and I and even our grandchildren are long gone. Thank you for listening patiently to me. I am truly grateful and feeling much lighter now after divulging the secret and eternal mystery of that haunted palace. Thank you so much, and by the way, my apologies for not asking you earlier, "What is your good name?"

The Apartment on the Tenth Floor

Nisha woke up with a sudden start and sat on her bed. She could hear the sound of muffled footsteps in the hall. She looked beside her and noticed Naresh lying on the bed in his deep slumber, snoring peacefully. The fluorescent hands of the table clock by her bedside showed 2:30 AM. Sudden thoughts crept into her mind. Had she imagined something? She sat there for a while, thinking what had she heard, and then she heard the soft rustling noise once again. Someone was stealthily walking in the hall.

"Ravi, sweetheart, are you thirsty?" she called out loud. There was no answer. "He must be asleep, but I better check." She got out of bed and slowly felt her way in the darkness along the passage which opened into their master bedroom, kitchen, bathroom and into the second bedroom up ahead, where the boy slept. She called out again, this time in a softer tone. "Ravi was it you I heard walking in the…," she stopped short as she looked at the bed in Ravi's room. It was empty. The bed sheet was rumpled and the blanket lay tossed aside. She had just passed the bathroom and there was no one there either. Where was Ravi?

Alarmed, she came out in the hall. The gossamer curtains were filtering in the lights from the society's well lit common area below. Their apartment was on the sixth floor but the light coming in was still sufficient for discerning the dark shapes of the sofa, chairs, centre table, TV and dining table. Nisha stood in the hall, fear now gripping her senses. She suddenly noticed the front door. It was ajar!

"Oh my god, where has he gone at this hour," she shrieked and ran back to wake up Naresh. She shook Naresh violently and he got up, still groggy with sleep. When he finally made sense of what his wife was blabbering, he sprang out of the bed and they ran out of the apartment into the lift lobby. There was no one there. Nisha began to sob. "Look! He's gone below," Naresh stared at the lift panel display. It showed 'G' - for ground floor, that lit brightly in red, indicating where the lift had stopped last. "Come on, from the stairs."

When the Mishras reached the ground floor huffing and out of breath, they were totally shocked by the sight which greeted them. In the waiting area of the entrance lobby, their eleven-year-old son was sitting on the sofa, his head drooping a little. But what puzzled them most was that Ravi was dressed in his school uniform, had the backpack on his shoulders and was tightly clutching the strap of his water bottle.

~~~

"Ravi," a nurse in a white sari called out. "Ravi Mishra," she repeated with a louder voice. In the large waiting hall of Dr Potnis Child Clinic, a couple sprang up to their feet and responded to the call. They hurriedly entered the consulting room and took their seats. The nurse closed the door and stood there.

"It's a case of somnambulism or commonly known as sleep walking," remarked the bespectacled doctor smiling affably. "It is something very common among children in the age group 6-12. Sometimes it runs in the family, I mean a genetic trait." he paused looking inquiringly. "Nothing to worry about, it will go away as the child grows older."

"Would you prescribe any medicine that we need to give him? Or suggest any preventive measures?" Nisha asked. She had been ruefully upset since morning. "Not required at this stage," the doctor replied. "But you must take precautions. Sleep walkers are very much prone to injuries. They can bump into a wall or trip over a table. You have to be alert during nights as he has shown symptoms of sleep walking." The Mishras thanked the doctor and left.

When they stepped out of the clinic Naresh said to his wife in a consoling tone, "See, I had also told you the same. So, don't worry and relax. Just to be on the safer side, from now on we will have to lock the balcony and front door at night." Nisha nodded.

At the other end of the city, in an airy classroom, 35 children sat on wooden benches waiting for the last class of the day to end.

Ravi pulled out his pencil box and shared an eraser with a boy sitting next to him "Thanks Ravi," Gaurav said. "You always seem to have spares with you." The boys chuckled softly and turned their attention towards the board where the maths teacher had scribbled in tiny capital letters 'TRANSLATE INTO ALGEBRAIC EXPRESSION'. Ravi copied the words on his notebook and then gazed at the questions:

1) Six fifth of 'h' is subtracted from 3

2) 5 more than quotient of 'x' and 3.

Ravi let out a low groan. This was really boring. He whispered to Gaurav who was busy writing down the answers in his exercise book. "I hate algebra. I have still not understood why should we use alphabets in a maths class, and why do they keep changing the alphabets? Sometimes it is 'm' then 'x' and then 'h'." Just then, to Ravi's immense relief, the final bell rang. School was over for the day!

Later at home that evening, his parents told him of the sleep walking incident. As they had expected, he remembered nothing. "No Mom, I did not get up last night at all! I had a good sleep," Ravi protested. Nisha smiled dryly, "You did wake up and walk dear, anyways, after dinner I want you to study for your Science Olympiad."

"Yes, I will," said Ravi, slightly annoyed at being nagged constantly for his studies.

It was 10:30 PM when Ravi shut his book. He let out a long yawn and looked out of the sliding glass panes which opened into a tiny adjoining balcony. He had placed his study table to face the balcony, preferring to have his back to the room's door. The Mishras used to live on the sixth floor of Tower 1 in Sky Towers, the most marquee residential society in that part of the city. The Sky Towers were basically a 5-tower complex, built in a U shape, with Tower 1, 2 directly facing Tower 4, 5. Tower 3 was the perpendicular connecting building of the U. Each tower had sixteen floors and on each floor, there were three flats. The distance between the facing towers was about 25 meters, short enough to see fair amount of details but long enough to make faces of people moving about in the rooms unrecognizable.

It was still not dead of the night and most of the households had their lights on. It was such an amazing sight, Ravi felt. Small lighted squares, each one showing a different view of a different household, against the darkness of the night. He ran his eye through each vista – a family eating their dinner and watching TV, a man playing with his dog, a masked man pointing a gun at a couple, a housewife drawing the curtains, an old woman collecting dried clothes from… Ravi suddenly realized what he had seen. He quickly retraced his vision back to the apartment where the murder was about to unfold before his eyes! 'Bang, bang,' the masked man fired two shots into their heads and the couple slumped onto the floor. The man with the mask called out to his accomplices and in a moment they were gone. The blood spread slowly across the floor…and then it became all dark. Ravi could see no more. It turned out a dreary night and sleep dodged him for many hours, the visions repeatedly haunting him. He could not remember the hour when he finally fell asleep.

~~~

The next day dawned like any other and nothing unusual was noticed in and around Sky Towers. When Ravi reached home from school, he was surprised. There was no hullabaloo about the murder he had witnessed last night! "It must not have been discovered yet?" he shuddered at the memory of the last night. "I better keep mum," as he threw his bag on his bed and walked over out on the balcony. He cast a furtive look at the apartments in Tower 5 and tried to recall which one was it. "It was not one of the bordering ones, must be one of those in the middle," he muttered to himself, his finger tracing the circle to mark out the probable rooms.

"Ravi dear, have you changed your dress? Go and eat the fruits I have cut for you," Nisha called out from the kitchen. "And get ready quickly, we have to go to Parag Uncle's anniversary party."

The celebrations and unbridled mirth at the evening party made Ravi forget his dreadful memory of the night before and by the time they returned home, he was dead tired. Without changing his party-dress he sank in his bed. Nisha cleaned up the utensils, arranged things for tomorrow and shouted to him. "Come on lazy boy, get up and brush your teeth before you sleep." She also gestured to Naresh to secure the house-door in case Ravi got up in the night to sleep walk. When all was over, they retired to their bedroom.

Ravi got up grudgingly. He changed into his night-suit, brushed his teeth perfunctorily and returned sluggishly to doze off. Tomorrow would be another happy Saturday which meant no waking up early for the school bus. He switched off the lights, turned the fan regulator to maximum and was about to jump into his bed, when his gaze fell inadvertently on the array of apartments in the facing tower. Once more he was dazed by what he saw. He could see the same masked man pointing a gun at a couple. 'Bang, bang,' the masked man fired two shots into their heads and the couple slumped. The man with the mask called out to his accomplices and in a moment they were gone. The blood spread slowly across the floor...and then it became all dark.

Ravi shuddered. He was now totally aghast. He rubbed his eyes and pinched himself to see if he hadn't imagined it. He had seen exactly the same events repeat themselves in the living room of that apartment. Bewildered, he stood blankly staring at the dark room for a while. Finally, he said to himself, "It could be the effect of that sleep walking, a bad bout might have induced some hallucinations. It might freak out Mom even more." Ravi finally lay down and fell asleep.

And it became a routine affair beyond any plausible explanation. At around the same time every night, Ravi would see that gory event repeating itself in the same room of that opposite tower. It used to be all over within a few seconds. Ravi learnt to conveniently ignore the weird happenings. But one day the story made it to the newspapers.

~ ~ ~

"Mom, can you get me some jam. Don't feel like having butter on bread today."

"Well, only after you have finished the one in your plate."

"And finish it fast!" Naresh's head popped up from behind the newspaper he was reading. Ravi obeyed, and began munching the bread quickly. His eyes fell on the headline of the news article which read "*DENTIST COUPLE SHOT DEAD AT SHANTI KUNJ, ASSAILANTS FLEE.*"

Ravi read through the lines of the article and he slowly stopped eating, his hand still holding the bread.

"…Armed robbers wearing masks on their faces broke into Mr and Mrs Gurnani's residence and shot the couple point blank. Police are suspecting the gunman fired on the spur, and have ruled out premeditated murder. All the assailants are missing. When contacted on phone, Mr Gurnani's brother said…"

Ravi was shocked. The news report exactly described the scene he had witnessed every night inside the apartment in the opposite Tower! But what puzzled him most was the location. The newspaper reported it as Shanti Kunj and it was several miles away from Sky Towers. This was really baffling.

"I think I will have to speak to Gaurav about this today. He is smart," Ravi thought.

Gaurav and Ravi had been best friends since grade I. Their families knew each other well. They did not live too far apart either. Both the boys often met each other in the evening to play tennis in the Sky Towers' court. Gaurav's parents often allowed him to stay over at Ravi's place over the weekend.

"Hmm, that's quite a coincidence!" said Gaurav. It was lunch break and the boys were sitting on the bench in the shade of the neem trees. "But how do you explain the same scene repeating itself over and over again?" asked Ravi. "That is definitely weird, may be you did imagine all this."

Ravi's face fell and seeing his forlorn expression, Gaurav patted his back. "Hey, don't worry friend. It has got nothing to do with your sleep walking business. My cousin also sleepwalks but never sees imaginary things. Don't mix these two things up. Cheer up and don't put so much stress on your mind. Save that for the afternoon algebra class. Mr Omair, I hear, has been planning a surprise test before the mid-term exams begin!"

Ravi let out a groan and held his head in his hands. Gaurav laughed out loud.

The boys spent the next few days rigorously preparing for the exams. Ravi went to school, came back and studied late into the night. Lately, his dad used to sit with him every night helping with maths and science. Meantime Ravi had one or two minor episodes of sleep walking but it was improving, much to the relief of his parents. The boys often met in the evenings but their conversations revolved around topics limited to mid-term exams, papers, the brats at school, Mr Omair and algebra.

It was the night prior to his last exam, when Ravi again witnessed action in the apartment. Only, this time, it was a different scene altogether!

~~~

"Nisha, at what time is Vikram's flight landing in India?" Naresh called out to his wife, loosening the tie. "Your brother is busier than my global CEO, so I better book an appointment right now," he quipped.

Nisha took it lightly, hit her husband on his back with clenched fist and replied with animated sarcasm, "Of course he is, after all he is my kid brother. Mr Mishra, you may fix the appointment at 9:00 PM tomorrow night at the airport. No reschedules are allowed."

"Ok, dear, done!"

Nisha gave a loving smile and hurried to clean up the dinner leftovers. Naresh had come late from office and they had their dinner immediately. She peeped inside Ravi's room and said "Sonny, Vicky uncle will be coming over tomorrow, so we need to receive him at the airport. Have you finished your readings for tomorrow's history paper?"

"Yes, Mom, I have. I wish Vicky uncle gets me something terrific this time. Even Gaurav is eagerly waiting to know what gift I'll get this year!" Ravi beamed with expectation.

"Ha ha… yes. Ok, quick, go to sleep. After your exams, we'll go to the supermarket and stack up the house. Tomorrow is going to be a real fun day."

"Yippee… good night Mom!"

"Sleep well dear."

Ravi lay awake tossing and turning in his bed. It was always difficult to sleep on the night before the exams. There was so much neural activity that shutting the brain down was difficult. He got up, dragged his chair into the balcony and sat down. But for the dim light emitted from the starlit sky overhead, it was dark and silence prevailed. All the apartments in the front tower were engulfed in semi-darkness. Most of them were shielded by heavy curtains hung from the pelmets. There was a gentle breeze blowing in from the open side of the U shaped building complex.

A light suddenly lit up in one of the rooms and it caught Ravi's attention. In another instant, Ravi recognized this was the same room of the murder scene! He watched intently, expecting the masked gunman to appear. But nothing like that happened. To his surprise, a tall, lanky man wearing nothing but shorts was visible. He seemed to be agitated about something as he paced up and down the room. The man stopped suddenly, as if he had made up his mind about something, and disappeared into the inner room. Ravi waited patiently. In a moment, he reappeared with a long rope knotted into a circular noose at one end. The man dragged a plastic stool, placed it in the centre of the room and stood on it. He then tied the other end of the rope in the hook of the ceiling fan, pulled it with both hands and tested its strength. Now he slipped the noose around his neck and kicked the stool away. Just about five minutes later the desperate kicking of his legs stopped and his body hung limp, twisting slowly under its own weight. Looking from the balcony of his house, Ravi shook and shivered with cold fear. He hastily retreated in his room, slid the glass doors shut and pulled his blanket over his head. Still horrified, he dared not to open his eyelids. Minutes ticked away and finally he was asleep.

Next day at school, the history paper was tough but still Ravi came out beaming from the examination hall. He had made up his mind to catch Gaurav but he could not find him in the melee of the celebrations among students who were thrilled now that the exams were over. Nisha picked him up from the school and they spent the rest of the day shopping. Vikram's flight landed on time and by 10:30 PM they were home.

"Ravi, guess what I brought for you this time?" Vikram slid his hand inside the oversized bag and took out a large box, and held it out invitingly for Ravi to inspect.

"Play station."

"No."

"Skates."

"No."

"Err... then I cannot guess, let me open it," his eyes gleaming with excitement, Ravi snatched the box and hastily tore open the packaging. Inside he saw the picture on the box and squealed with delight "Binoculars! Yahhhhoooo," he sprang forward and hugged uncle tightly.

"Ok now, Ravi let your uncle take rest, he had a long flight and has important meetings to attend tomorrow," said Naresh.

"Sure, thanks uncle, this is the best gift I could have asked for," Ravi put the lenses to his eyes and ran off to call Gaurav.

"Arre, where did you disappear after the exams, I wanted to talk to you. How did the paper go, could you finish all questions?" Ravi spoke in the landline's receiver. His parents forbade him to carry his own cell phone, which annoyed Ravi a lot, as all his friends had one.

(Pause)

"Oh I see, cool, hey uncle bought me a pair of binoculars from the US."

(Pause)

"Yes they are really powerful. Want to test them out in the zoo."

(Pause)

GRAVEYARD SHIFT

"No, not tomorrow, but I will let you know when we can go. Hey, before you hang up, I wanted to tell you something else as well." Ravi looked around. He saw dad and uncle in deep conversation, while mom was in the bedroom. He lowered his voice and whispered,

"About that apartment in the opposite Tower. I have seen another strange happening yet again last night. Not the usual gunman murdering the couple this time, but a man hanging himself!" There was a long pause as Ravi listened intently to the voice which came from the other side.

"Yea, ok, let's catch up soon and discuss. At least I am glad you are taking this seriously. Good Night." Ravi put the phone down.

Something intuitive told Ravi he would be seeing the hanging man again tonight, and on many more nights to come. As he stood looking, a thought came to him, "Would I see the scene during day time also? I will surely check out over this weekend." After waiting for twenty minutes, Ravi went about tidying his room, but kept an intermittent vigil on the opposite Tower. It was around 11:15 PM when he saw it! The man stood on a plastic stool, tied the other end of the rope in the hook of the ceiling fan, tested it for its strength, slipped the noose around his neck and kicked the stool away. Just five minutes later the desperate kicking of the legs stopped and the body hung limp, twisting slowly under its own weight. Then all went blank and it became dark again.

Ravi stood in his balcony deeply pondering. His eyes were still transfixed at the dark square room which a moment ago, was lit up. A thought occurred to him. He marked out the room with his left index finger and began counting the floors from the ground. Three, Four… Eight, Nine, Ten. "Ten it is," Ravi said out aloud. "There would be three flats on the tenth floor, so need to work out which one of the three this one is. Gaurav, my friend, I would need your help in sorting the mystery behind the apartment on the tenth floor."

~~~

The next morning Ravi woke up early. He wanted to check the apartment in daylight. While brushing his teeth, he stepped out in the balcony and counted up to ten from below. Once his vision was at the tenth floor, it was fairly easy to locate the room. Ravi was surprised to see it was completely empty! It had absolutely nothing, bare walls only, no furniture and not even any fans hanging from the ceiling. It appeared no one had ever lived in that apartment. "This is getting really weird," Ravi blabbered incoherently due to the toothbrush under his tongue. "I am going to sit out all day here if required and check if the scene repeats itself during the day."

Nisha did not require much convincing when her son proposed he wanted to spend the day sitting in the balcony reading the books brought by Vicky uncle from the US. She was glad he would be out of her way. With his vacations begun, he usually turned out to be quite a handful to manage. "Why don't you bring Gaurav over as well? I can leave you boys in the house and get my work done," she suggested. Ravi jumped up at this offer and nodded his head gleefully.

"So, that's it?" Gaurav said when Ravi pointed his finger at the apartment. Following his mother's suggestion Ravi had quickly called Gaurav who was also happy to come over since his parents were out to do shopping for a family wedding. Gaurav hated shopping and felt uneasy in presence of a crowd. By afternoon, his parents had dropped him at the gate of Sky Towers saying that they will pick him back in the evening. Nisha was also not there. She too had left with Naresh and Vikram. The boys were thankful to have the house to themselves and were standing in the balcony adjoining Ravi's room.

"Yes, and as you can see, it is completely empty," Ravi remarked emphatically, standing with his hands placed on his hips.

"Let us start with finding which apartment that is."

"And how do we find that out?"

"Simple, just go on the tenth floor and ring the doorbell. 2 out of 3 doors will open, the one which does not will be the apartment we are looking for," Gaurav said casually. Ravi looked at him in awe and silently admitted his logic. "He is amazing."

"Let's go then," and the boys ran out. Ravi locked the outer door of their apartment and slid the bunch of keys in his pocket.

The boys took the lift down to the ground floor and stepped out into the society's common area. The swimming pool was full and kids were yelping around in the water. Ravi and Gaurav walked down the pavement and reached the lobby of Tower 5. The security personnel manning Tower 5's reception lobby were busy chatting with the society plumber, and the boys quickly slipped into the lift and pressed 10.

Floor 10 was no different and looked exactly like any other floor in Sky Towers. As the lift-door opened the boys got out and came across the 3 apartments 1001, 1002 and 1003, embossed on the shining brass plates.

"We don't need to ring the doorbells at all. Look," Gaurav pointed to the apartment 1003 which was towards the right of the lift landing. Ravi also looked at the door of 1003, but could not infer anything. He turned back to Gaurav and inquired "What do you mean?"

"Can't you see dumb head, both 1001 and 1002 have name plates, the litter-bins have just been cleared and doormats are worn out from regular use. Now look at 1003 and what do you see?" Ravi looked again at the door of 1003.

"Nothing! You are right, as always. That is the apartment which I see from my room. Come let's have a closer look."

The boys tip-toed to the door and stood there. They looked at each other. A sense of unease crept up their senses. Ravi was the first to speak "Isn't it very cold here?"He wrapped his arms around his chest. "That is very strange." He looked at Gaurav and could see he was feeling the chill as well. "Hey! look at the door," Gaurav remarked suddenly and that startled Ravi. "A hole has been drilled into the wood, but no glass lens has been fitted in that peephole. Wow! Isn't it something strange! It's apparent that this flat is vacant since the building was built. Let me see what is in there. Give me a hand, will you?"

Ravi bent down and clasped Gaurav's legs firmly. Then he heaved and raised Gaurav several inches, enough for Gaurav to quickly put his right eye on the eyehole. "Ouch!" Gaurav let out a low wail and pushed himself away from the eyehole. Ravi loosened his clasp. "What happened, did you see anything scary?"

"Phew… it is freezing cold in there man! Look at my right eye, I got such a blast of frigid air in my eye that it's hurting."

"Weird, why is it so cold in there!"

"And there is nothing inside. In fact, the construction was left halfway. I could see that the left side walls have not even been plastered. No ceiling fans are there, hence no chance for committing suicide by hanging." Gaurav said while rubbing his eye. It had truly become red and water was trickling from it.

"Come, let's get back to our house. I don't like to be here anymore." Ravi said.

"Me too."

As they were passing by the lobby on the ground floor, Ravi nudged Gaurav to stop. He was looking at the display of name plates on the wall showing the flat numbers and their respective owners. 1003 was missing!

The boys were puzzled. They quietly returned to Ravi's house. Nisha had not returned yet and the boys helped themselves earnestly from the well-stocked refrigerator. Ravi took out two cans of Coke and some Swiss chocolates which Vicky uncle had brought. They turned the TV, flipped a few channels, and soon got bored. Ravi turned to Gaurav and said, "So, what's next?"

Gaurav looked at him but did not respond immediately. He finished munching the chocolate, got up, threw the wrapper in the dustbin and slumped on the bean bag. "Are you sure you did not imagine this all up? The apartment is empty! No one has ever lived in there."

"What rubbish you are talking about! Do you think I am mad," Ravi retorted vehemently.

"Although I think you are," Gaurav said mischievously, "but it is still not clear to me why only you among hundreds living in this society are seeing these 10 sec horrific video clips in the night."

"Ok in that case you need to stay with me tonight and see those damn things with your own eyes," Ravi said angrily.

"Hey, I need to meet my…"

"Nothing doing, my friend. I am going to call your mom right now and arrange everything."

And so it was arranged. After a couple of pleading phone calls from Ravi, Gaurav's parents allowed him to stay over for the night at Ravi's place. The only consideration which required some thought was Ravi's sleepwalking. But they gave in and Ravi had his way. Naresh and Vikram were going to be home late, so Nisha suggested the boys to have their dinner early and pack off to their room for the night. They settled themselves in the balcony and chatted away till around 11 PM when Ravi jumped up suddenly.

"Look, there it begins, look."

Gaurav looked in the direction of Ravi's outstretched arm and viewed the scene, so vividly described to him before. A tall, lanky man wearing nothing but shorts stood on a plastic stool, tied the other end of the rope in the hook of the ceiling fan, tested it for its strength, slipped the noose around his neck and kicked the stool away. Just 5 minutes later the desperate kicking of the legs stopped and his body hung limp, twisting slowly under its own weight.

Gaurav let out a deep sigh and sat down heavily.

The two boys did not linger around in the balcony any longer. There was a nip in the air, and they came inside, slid the glass panes shut and got in the bed. Laying side by side they chatted for a while, without any reference to the mysterious enactment they had seen and then fell asleep. By that time, the other members of the Mishra household had already dined and were fast asleep. Vikram was staying with his in laws tonight.

Towards early morning, it happened once again. Ravi began to sleep walk!

His eyes were open, but bereft of any expression. He got out of the bed noiselessly, and strangely headed for the kitchen. His gait was slow, heavy, his head drooping forward a little as he drifted in to the dark passage and then into the kitchen. The light from the hall cast over eerie shadows in the passageway. For the next few minutes, he just stood in the kitchen aimlessly, still asleep but eyes wide open.

Ever since the first episode of sleep walking, Nisha never slept soundly. She knew her husband would sleep undisturbed even during an earthquake, so she had developed a habit to wake up at the slightest noise emanating from Ravi's room, and even otherwise, she used to get up at least 3 times in the night to check on her son. Tonight, however, she had taken a pill and Ravi's prowling had gone unnoticed.

In the kitchen, Ravi's hand stretched forward and grasped an apple from the fruit-basket kept on the slab. He pulled at a trolley and it slid open noiselessly. He groped around and soon found it, a sharp kitchen knife. It was only when he picked up a steel plate from the lower trolley, the clanging noises became loud enough to disturb Nisha and Gaurav's sleep. Nisha woke up instantly, while Gaurav just changed this side.

"Oh shit, he must be walking again. Wake up, quickly!" Nisha said aloud as she gave Naresh a violent shove. She did not, however, wait for Naresh to respond. She jumped out of her bed without any further delay and switched on the passageway light. She hurriedly reached the kitchen and stopped short. There was Ravi, his eyes blankly staring at the front, while his hands went on cutting the apple in an awkward clumsy manner. It was then that Nisha noticed the awkwardly cut pieces of apple were daubed in deep crimson and lying in a pool of blood in the steel plate. Ravi had cut his fingers deep.

~~~

"I was repeatedly telling you that we should lock the door of his room from outside every night," a tearful Nisha shouted to her husband. She had just finished cleaning and bandaging the wounds. There were three deep cuts which needed proper dressing. By then Gaurav had also woken up. Ravi was crying, as the wounds were painful.

"That does not help in any way Nisha," Naresh thundered back, "He can hurt himself in his room as well. Locking him in is not the solution. Anyway, we can talk about that later, you stay at home with Gaurav, I am going to rush him to the 24 x 7 child emergency centre."

Later that day, they all sat in the living room. It was a holiday and Vikram had returned to check on his nephew. Gaurav had returned to his home. The family discussed the best approach to make Ravi accident proof from his sleep walking but no effective conclusion could be reached as Nisha was still emotionally disturbed. The men decided to let time pass by.

As far as Ravi was concerned, he remembered nothing. "Why the hell would I be cutting apples in the middle of the night?" he had wondered. In a day he soon forgot about it as the pain in his fingers subsided. He turned his attention back on the apartment on the tenth floor. There were still a few days for school to reopen. Gaurav had gone on vacation with his family and the boys were out of touch. Uncle Vicky left for another city on a business trip but promised to be back in a week. Surreptitiously Ravi continued to keep a close vigil on the apartment during the days but never ever saw the hanging man; however he almost always saw him between 10 and 11:30 PM. It was the night before the school opened again, that Ravi got the biggest shock of his life.

"How's your finger now, dear," Nisha asked from the dinner table. She usually ate after Ravi had finished his meal.

"Fully healed," Ravi remarked showing his fingers to her.

"Very good. So it's school from tomorrow! Need to get up early again," she smiled.

"Yea, I know," Ravi let out a dismal groan.

"Before you sleep, please clean up your room."

"Ok, mom."

Ravi got about cleaning his room. He picked up his scattered clothes and heaved them in a plastic bin. Then his eyes fell on the binoculars which Vicky uncle had gifted. An idea struck him. "Maybe I should use these powerful lenses to see the scene in that apartment. I would be able to see the man very clearly, even his face."

He looked at the wall clock; it was ten minutes past ten. He quickly tidied up his room in the next few minutes, took the binoculars and sat down in the chair on the balcony. When Nisha dropped in, she did not question him, as the assigned task had been completed to her satisfaction. She simply asked him to go to bed in time and left.

At about quarter to eleven, the room suddenly lit up. Ravi knew it had begun. He put his binoculars to his eyes and tried to focus correctly. He had not used the binoculars before and struggled to get the image right. By the time his experimentations with the aperture size and focal length had succeeded, the scene was almost over. The man was hanging limp now. It was then that Ravi saw the man's face. His pulse quickened and hairs sprang straight at the back of his neck. Goosebumps surfaced all over his body. In the pale yellow light of the room, he could clearly see the dead body of Mr Omair, their maths teacher, hanging limp from the ceiling.

~~~

"What!" shrieked Gaurav "Are you sure it was our man Omi?"

"100% sure, cannot mistake his dreadful face with that reddish stubble. It was him all right," Ravi replied. The boys were sitting on their benches waiting for the first class of the day to begin. He was about to say something when the children sitting near the door rose and like a Mexican wave the rest of the class also stood up to greet the teacher.

A tall, lanky man with a reddish beard walked in briskly and the children spoke in unsynchronized unison, "Good Morning Sir."

Mr Tayyab Omair acknowledged the greeting without any expression on his face and gestured the class to sit down. Ravi looked spellbound at Omair as he grimly went about copying something from the textbook on to the blackboard. Ravi leaned and whispered in Gaurav's ear, "100% sure, it was our man Omi whom I saw hanging himself in the apartment on the tenth floor."

GRAVEYARD SHIFT

It was in the recess hours that Ravi asked Gaurav to come over to his house and see for himself. "Sorry chum, it'll not be possible anytime during this week," said Gaurav "May be over the weekend."

Both remained silent for a while. Children ran past them in the corridor where the boys stood. Ravi spoke first "Can you figure out what does this mean?"

"Honestly, I have no clue," Gaurav remarked. Then he turned to Ravi with a resolute expression on his face and said exasperatedly, "Look, let's forget this whole weird business. If we can't figure this out, we should just chuck it."

Ravi let out a muffled half-hearted affirmation in a disconcerted manner and looked at the lush green football field in the outer compound. Somehow he nurtured a premonition that the weird business had only just begun and Gaurav would have to eat his own words. It took only 24 hours for his hunch to come out true.

The weather on the next day turned out to be outright gloomy with dark clouds covering the city sky. The class had just come back from a strenuous session in the field, and the students had sunk in their chairs wiping the flowing perspiration off their foreheads, when the news came. A boy came streaking in and shouted out to the surprised students "Did any of you hear the breaking news? Omair sir killed himself last night." A wave of shock accompanied by rising murmurs and excited chatter filled the classroom. Sensing the source of information to be someone outside, all the students ran out. There were only two boys who did not budge an inch. Ravi and Gaurav were glued to their seats, stunned, looking dazed at each other.

And then the rumour mill began to run with all earnestness. The news of the maths teacher's shocking death spread like wildfire. Within minutes, Ravi and Gaurav overheard that last piece of corroboration they could have wanted to know. Tayyab Omair was wearing only his shorts when his body was found hanging from the ceiling.

~~~

"That room predicted and depicted Omair sir's death several days before," said Gaurav. He rubbed his chin, took a sip of the lemonade which Nisha had prepared for the boys. They were sitting in the collonaded park of Sky Towers. "Don't forget the murder of the dentist couple by the masked man. And the room has stopped replaying the scenes now that the event has actually happened. It's been four days now and I have never seen Omair sir's hanging body again," Ravi added in.

"Hmm," Gaurav stood there in afternoon sun engrossed in deep thought. Ravi knew that some concrete action would surely come out of such introspection and he was absolutely correct. Gaurav asked purposefully, "You got a piece of paper, something to scribble on?"

Ravi had none, but saw some local internet company's advertising leaflets flitting around in the gentle breeze. He sprinted and soon caught hold of one. Gaurav already had a pencil out. He took the paper, sat down on a park-bench and began scribbling intently.

Over his shoulder, Ravi saw he was writing down something in the form of a questionnaire. After a few minutes, Gaurav paused. He glanced at what he had written and then read out aloud.

1. Why has no one else in Sky Towers seen the scenes?

2. Why does it always happen at night?

3. Why Apartment 1003, why not in any other apartment?

"Anything else you can think of?"

"Yes, you forgot the most important point. How do we find answers to all these questions?" Ravi replied humorously with a mocking seriousness.

Gaurav smiled heartily. "Yes, you are right, buddy. But I know where to start."

"And that would be?" Ravi raised his eyebrows inquiringly.

"Uncle Vicky!"

"What… are you crazy? Mom is already freaking out on my nightly sleepwalking adventures and you want to drive her delirious with this."

GRAVEYARD SHIFT

"Relax, you are so straight Ravi, learn to be a little crooked, a little smart sometimes." Gaurav said shaking his head. "I remember you had mentioned to me that Uncle Vicky has friends in the US who are known to be paranormal investigators."

Ravi went silent for a moment and thought "There he goes again."

Gaurav folded the piece of paper and pocketed it. With a long swig from the glass, he finished the drink, wiped his mouth and remarked "Leave it to me. Let's think this out."

Over the next couple of hours, the two boys cooked up a story for telling uncle Vikram. Ravi would first create circumstances so as to catch his uncle when no one would be around except them. Vikram knew Gaurav, so it would be easier for Gaurav to spin the cock and bull story of his cousin living in the South who sees premonitions of death in an apartment tower facing the one in which he lives. Ravi would be replaced with the imaginary cousin, rest everything would remain the same. Gaurav would slyly and carefully place a hint before Vikram whether it would be possible for him to ask if his friends in US could help and clarify as to what was happening. They set the plan in action the following day and were surprised to see how easily it worked. Vikram had no faintest idea in his mind about their hidden plan and did not suspect anything; on the contrary, he was happy to show off his interest and connections that could throw light on the mystery of Gaurav's story. The boys exchanged smiles, as he opened his laptop and typed a mail to his friend in the US.

"Ok there you go," Vikram said, "It is still night in the US, so we should get Eric's reply by late evening or night. I will let you know what he has to say on this."

"Thank you so much uncle. You are amazing. One more request, can we keep this to the three of us only? Our folks would go berserk if they found out we are poking our noses in areas other than studies and sports," Gaurav said with a twinkle in his eye.

"Ha ha," Vikram laughed, "Oh, sure I won't tell anyone."

Even though uncle had promised to be silent, Ravi was careful not to broach the topic of the email when his parents were at home.

He went to bed without asking Vikram if any reply had come. Meanwhile, the apartment on the tenth floor had remained silent since the day of Tayyab Omair's death. Ravi had seen nothing for several days now, in spite of his strict vigil.

The next day was a national holiday, and school was closed. Vikram was going to pay a visit to them in the evening and Ravi hoped to catch him then. It was a hot morning and Ravi was in the swimming pool. From the pool he could see the entire U of Sky Towers. His thoughts again went back to the mysterious apartment, when some idea flashed in his mind. He stood in the waist deep cool water, slowly moving his hands. "Let me give it a try, nothing to lose," he thought.

He got out of the pool, took a quick shower and dressed up. He walked briskly up to the security guard of Tower 5 and slumped on the sofa, showing how much tired he was after spending all that time in the swimming pool. The conversation started from trivial things, Ravi remembered how Gaurav used his uncanny craft to make people start talking. After the topics like weather forecasts, milkman's irregularity and frequent lift breakdown were done with, Ravi saw his moment and slipped in the question he wanted to ask. Pointing to the name plate, he asked casually, "Why is there no 1003?"

Ravi observed the guard's face closely. It was to check if there was any change in expression at that question. The security guard just shrugged his shoulders and smiled. Apparently, this was a question he had answered several times before. He replied nonchalantly, "The builder never completed the construction of that flat and it was never sold."

"Oh, why did they abandon the work?"

"No idea, this building was completed 4 years back. I was not employed here then. But I heard from someone that there was the problem of Vaastu with that particular flat."

"Problem of what?" Ravi asked.

"Vaastu," the security guard repeated. The phone on his desk rang and he got busy attending to the caller.

Ravi got up and strolled out. When he reached his house, Nisha was busy with preparing lunch. He sat before the computer and typed the words 'Vaastu' in Google search box. He glanced through the string of results, and clicked on one of the links which appealed to him. He read on…

…is an ancient doctrine which consists of precepts born out of a traditional view on how the laws of nature affect human dwellings…

…The Vaastu Purusha Mandala is an indispensable part of vaastu shastra and constitutes the mathematical and diagrammatic basis for generating design. It is the metaphysical plan of a building that incorporates the coarsely bodies and supernatural forces. Purusha refers to energy, power, soul or cosmic man. Mandala is the generic name for any plan or chart which symbolically represents the cosmos…

Ravi gave it up and closed the window. He could not understand a single word he had read. He decided to wait till the evening for Uncle Vicky's return. At 7 PM, the doorbell rang. Ravi ran to open it and to his delight found the person he was waiting for. He hugged Vikram, immaculately dressed in his Savile Row suit. Sensing his nephew's excitement, he whispered in Ravi's ear, "Got a response, very interesting. I have a printout of the email, will give you later." Ravi could not wait further to go through the email from Uncle Vicky's friend. When he finally got his hands on the print out, he rushed to his room, closed the door and went through it quickly. "This is amazing. I need to show this to Gaurav tomorrow. He would surely make more sense out of this than I can." With one last look at the apartment on the tenth floor, which was dark and quiet, he went to sleep.

The next day, before the morning assembly at the school, Ravi got hold of Gaurav and excitedly shoved the printout in his hand. "Go through this! Reply has come from uncle's friend and I cannot tell you how incredible the whole thing sounds."

Gaurav read it aloud, albeit in a low voice, so that no one else could listen.

My Dear Vikram

I am doing very fine. Nancy and I moved to a new house over the weekend, (don't worry, it is not far from your place). Been really busy settling down, getting the kids adjusted to the new place etc. they did not like it initially, but getting settled a bit.

I am surprised (and happy also in a way) to get your mail. You seem to have got messed up there with supernatural entities and spooky apartments! Welcome to the club buddy. When you are back here, come with me on one of our investigative tours. It'll be fun.

Now to your story and questions which you have put forward. It clearly appears to be a case of a "crossover." In our supernatural lingo, a crossover is basically a physical place where the plane of the spirit world crosses the plane of the living world. Think of it as two lines which ideally should never touch, forget cross each other, but due to a freak, unexplained cause, they intersect each other. Now, since crossovers are a rare anomaly (I call it bad design of nature by god), they usually attract intense paranormal activity, especially of the negative kind. Consequently, most of the sightings are of a violent nature; evil spirits, demonic possessions or more commonly premonitions of gruesome murder, suicide, horrific accidents. Crossovers can occur anywhere, from deep inside underwater caves, frigid snow-capped mountains to your nondescript neighbourhood mom & pop store. That apartment you mentioned seems to me is one such example of a crossover. Oh and by the way, there is some tell-tale sign associated with a crossover place. Such place could be unusually dark in spite of being in a sunny or lighted environment; or it would be stinking badly; or it could be very, very cold almost freezing. Did that apartment show any of these signs?

Gaurav paused and let out a low whistle. Ravi nodded his head. He remembered the cold sensation they had felt standing outside the apartment. Gaurav continued reading:

In regard to your questions like 'why don't other people see the scenes in the apartment,', 'why those become visible only at night'; honestly, I have no clue. I can hazard a wild guess about electromagnetic waves getting stronger in the night time but let's leave it at that. We do not understand these phenomena. Crossovers are quite difficult to find, in fact, in my 15 year stint as a paranormal investigator, I have come across them only on 3 occasions. We know very little about them.

Hope that helps :-) Actually, if we can get some solid evidences from this apartment — something like a video recording of the death premonitions — it would be of terrific help for my research. At the cost of sounding selfish, could it be possible for the boy you mentioned who was seeing this phenomenon to catch it on camera, upload on YouTube and send the link to me?

Rest all is well. When will you be back? Your promotion party is still due.

Cheerio,
Eric

"That is exactly what we are going to do," Gaurav snapped his fingers.

"But where do we get a camera from?" Ravi asked.

"No worries buddy, I have one at home. We just need to figure out how to get the tripod and the camera into your balcony in a way your folks don't suspect anything."

"If you can get uncle to write to his friend, I am certain you can also manage this small task easily," Ravi smiled.

"As a matter of fact, this is too easy for me," Gaurav laughed. The English teacher, a grey haired lady, walked in briskly and the boys shut up.

By the weekend, the boys had managed to convince and install the camera on a tripod in Ravi's balcony. The story presented before the parents this time was that they were learning how to use a DSLR camera as an extra-curricular project at school. The reference of school made the story more credible and also achieved the one thing they really wanted, to be left alone. Nisha and Naresh were also pleased to see their son doing something constructive during his free time.

"So this it set now. Look, I shot a sample video clip and you can see the apartment clearly. Don't touch the zoom dial anymore," Gaurav announced after spending several tiring minutes getting the expensive camera set to auto-focus mode to get sharp pictures of the apartment in question.

"I just need to charge the batteries during the day, slot them in around 9:30 PM, start the video recording and stop it after the scene gets over or otherwise by 12:00 PM," Ravi repeated the instructions he had received.

"Correct. Now come on, help me haul this polythene cover across the top. That would protect the expensive lens in case it rains. Don't want dad to get angry."

The apartment had been silent since several days now. Ravi did not even know whether it would light up again and play forth another gruesome death scene. Three uneventful days rolled by. Every night Ravi set the video recording on at 9:30. He kept a lookout as well but when nothing showed up, he stopped the camera at about 12. And then on the fourth night, when Ravi had lost all hope, the room finally came alive!

A surge of adrenaline rushed through his body. Ravi checked if the camera was on, and seeing the green light blink, heaved a reassured sigh. He was intently looking at the apartment, when his dad burst into his room. Ravi turned instantly and saw that dad looked very worried.

"Ravi, go and sit beside your mom. She is crying. We need to leave right now for grandma's village. She wants all her near and dear ones by her side. And also help me with the packing."

Ravi could guess what had happened. His maternal grandmother, aged 81, had not been keeping well lately. Her time was near. He rushed to his mom and finding him by her side she embraced him tightly. She was speechless and her body trembled. Seeing his mom sobbing, he also could not hold back his tears.

In the middle of the night, the Mishras hurriedly packed their suitcases with what they could find at hand. Naresh had decided to drive down the 300 km journey. In a last minute hurried check, he made sure that they had shut all windows, locked the kitchen door leading to the dry area and switched off all fans. He had a feeling it would be sometime before they returned back from the village. "Ravi, I think I forgot your room's balcony door. Can you run and shut it securely?"

Ravi had completely forgotten about the camera which was still recording. Apartment 1003 had fallen silent long time back, but that consideration was hardly in Ravi's mind now. He quickly stopped the recording, folded the tripod assembly and dumped those on his bed. Then he slid the glass doors shut and heard the locks click automatically into the groove. He threw one last look at the Tower in front and ran back into the hall where his parents were waiting. At about 1 PM, their Honda Accord's engine whined and roared to life in the basement parking of Sky Towers. In another minute, the sedan sped away on the city highways, slowly melting in the night's darkness.

~~~

This same night, around the same time, another household was awake. They too had a problem at hand.

Madhuri Tyagi carefully removed the thermometer from beneath her son's tongue and held it obliquely so she could see the silvery mercury. "102.5 Fahrenheit," she exclaimed anxiously. Gaurav moaned and turned to his side. "The medicine will control the fever. Let us wait for another 30 mins," Ashish, her husband said.

"But we need to take him to the hospital, the very first thing in the morning," Madhuri said.

"Yes, look at him, he is shivering."

At the crack of dawn, Ashish picked up Gaurav from his bed. He was still running high temperature and had belched out the dinner taken last night. Tiny red dots had also appeared on his chest and abdomen.

By evening Gaurav was admitted. The doctor suspected dengue or malaria. They carried on the blood tests and when the reports came, it confirmed their primary suspicion – the blood platelet count reached a low of 70,000, indicating a possible severe infection due to dengue fever. And so Gaurav had to spend the next 7 days in the hospital battling with a stubborn fever which like an ominous grasp of Hydra sprang up again and again. His bones ached as if someone was hammering nails through them. The only thing he looked forward to was the visiting hours in the evening when his friends came to see him. Towards the end of his stay, when he was getting better and the fever was under control, he wondered why had Ravi not come to see him in the hospital. He had asked his parents to connect Ravi on the phone, but they firmly refused. They were afraid the two boys would be back again practicing their old habits which would put undue stress on Gaurav's fragile, recuperating body.

On the eighth day, Gaurav's unpleasant ordeal came to an end and the doctor signed his discharge papers. Gaurav could finally go home now, however attending school and games were still out of bounds. He had lost a lot of weight, was very weak and susceptible to infections, hence the diktat of complete bed rest was promptly announced. But he would have none! On the second day after his discharge, came that shattering piece of news. Gaurav's life was never going to be the same again.

It was a typical pleasant Sunday morning; the TV was on, telecasting devotional songs, his father was reading the newspaper while sipping a hot cup of coffee, his mom was tying her wet hair into a bun and he was lying in bed reading a Tintin comic when the phone had rung.

He did not notice his mom stroll lazily to the phone and pick it up, glaring at her husband who did not even care to look up from his paper. However, his attention was arrested the moment she shrieked wildly.

"WHAT!"

The person on the other end blurted something hurriedly.

"OH MY GOD!" screamed Madhuri. "OH MY GOD!" Gaurav put down what he was reading and looked in the direction of the hall. He could not see his parents as his room's door was shut. But he still heard his father jump from his seat and rush to mom's side. Madhuri was now wailing, tears streaked down her face.

"Yes, we must confirm the news first. Let me call up others. Give me a call immediately when you get more information," she said in a frail and choked voice. Gaurav could hear anxious, almost alarmed whispers between Madhuri and Ashish. He wondered why they were talking so softly. The morning dose of medicines made him feel dizzy and he closed his heavy eyelids, but sleep eluded him. In his semi-conscious state,he could not make sense of the nervous, frantic phone calls which his parents made continuously for the next couple of hours. It puzzled him, what could have happened to disrupt the pleasant ambience of such a peaceful bright morning!

By noon the news was confirmed and it spread like wildfire. It sent shock waves in their social circle. Friends and acquaintances outpoured their grief and utter disbelief at this unexpected sad news. Gaurav, still blissfully unaware, slept quietly in his bed though at heart he was eager to know what had happened. His friends called him, but Madhuri answered back saying Gaurav was asleep. They did not want to disturb him at the moment.

"We got to tell him," Ashish raised his glasses and rubbed his swollen eyes. Madhuri was still a nervous, crying wreck. There was a stinging pain in her head due to all that crying and non-stop phone calling.

"No, we should not. In this fragile state, he will break down even more."

"It is better we tell him rather than getting him to know about it from others. He has got to grow up and learn to accept such things."

"In that case I am NOT doing it. You do it," Madhuri relapsed into another bout of wailing.

"Ok I will, but stand beside me," Ashish said, being unsure about the fact that how his son would react to the news.

Madhuri nodded.

Gaurav felt a warm hand on his forehead. He opened his eyes and saw his dad smiling at him. "How are you feeling, my boy?" Ashish asked, throwing a quick glance at Madhuri who stood leaning by the wall.

"Much better, Papa. No fever," Gaurav smiled back weakly.

Ashish then spoke with a mellow firmness in his tone which he expected his son would identify and listen attentively, even in his illness.

"Son, there is some bad news. We just got to know it in the morning a few hours back."

"I know dad, I could figure out that something has gone wrong. What has happened?"

Ashish paused and looked at Madhuri for support, but she was not even looking at them. He cleared the lump in his throat, gave a deep sigh, and finally blurted it out.

"Ravi is no more. He was walking in his sleep when he fell to his death."

Gaurav stared blankly for a moment at his Dad. Madhuri turned her face just enough to catch her son's reaction. She was expecting an explosive outburst. Gaurav's reaction, however, surprised her. He just turned over to his side and slowly closed his eyes once again. Ashish looked up at his wife and shrugged his shoulders. They decided to let him come to terms with the import of the message at his own pace.

The next few days Gaurav silently cried and cried till his eyes turned sore. He had never cried so much in his life before, this was the worst feeling he had ever known. He was just unable to accept the fact that his best friend was gone forever. He resumed school but the talk all around there on the topic of Ravi's untimely demise just made him more miserable. Once in the classroom, the lead of his pencil broke, he immediately turned aside to ask for a spare and seeing the vacant chair next to him, burst out crying.

A pall of melancholic gloom had also descended on Sky Towers. Everyone went on talking about the shocking death of that adorable boy who lived on the sixth floor of Tower 1.

In the lift the fat woman said to her neighbour:

"I can't even dare to imagine the wretched condition of Nisha."

"I heard she has gone into severe mental depression and loses her senses intermittently. Hasn't yet shed a drop of tear and refuses to accept that her son is gone."

"Poor girl."

At the lobby entrance the two security men exchanged sad words:

"Such a nice boy he was."

"Used to walk in his sleep. Had even cut his finger on an earlier occasion."

GRAVEYARD SHIFT

In the swimming pool the children discussed the happening with glum faces.

"No, not in Sky Towers, it happened at his village."

"In the night?"

"Yes, when everyone else was asleep."

"This sleep walking is dangerous, scary too."

In the park the grandma said to others:

"I heard the man decided to quit his job and they are leaving the city for good."

"Yea, it must be unbearable to live here any longer."

"The mother needs psychiatric counselling."

~~~

It was a pleasant late evening two weeks after Ravi's premature and sad death, when the doorbell of Madhuri and Ashish Tyagi's residence rung. Gaurav was out for his drawing class and Madhuri was in the kitchen. Ashish rose to answer the door. A smartly dressed man was standing there. He looked a bit worn out and exhausted. He was carrying a tripod assembly and a camera.

"Hello."

"Hi, hello, you must be Mr Tyagi, Gaurav's father. I am Vikram, Ravi's maternal uncle."

"Oh please come in. How is err…" Ashish stopped short as the man's expression changed suddenly. He looked sullen and downcast. Ashish invited him in, "Please come in."

"No thanks, but I need to leave immediately. I just came to return this camera which I believe is yours. The boys were learning to experiment with it before…" he stopped as his eyes welled up.

Ashish felt a growing lump in his heart.

"Thank you Mr Tyagi. I shall take your leave now. Say my hello to Gaurav," Vikram said tearfully. Before Ashish could respond, he had turned his back and left.

With a despondent sigh and a shake of his head, Ashish closed the door.

When Gaurav came and saw the camera sitting invitingly on the tripod, the memories of his dear friend came flooding back. He remembered the days they sat talking of the apartment on the tenth floor, its gruesome scenes, the maths teacher, the email from Uncle Vicky's friend and their subsequent plan to video tape the bizarre scenes. All these were of no importance now. He did not care. Everything was over.

"We got to finish all packing tonight, nothing should be left for tomorrow," Madhuri said out loud at the dinner table. She and Ashish had decided to take Gaurav out for a short vacation. He had been feeling very lonely and glum since Ravi's death.

Ashish nodded excitedly to bring back a feeling of enjoyment, "Let me get the camera and charge the batteries first. Gaurav did you pack your rackets and skates?"

The family finished their packing by 1 AM. Tomorrow they would catch the flight at 10 AM. Madhuri was dead tired and she slept off immediately. Ashish was sitting before his laptop. He wanted to check if the batteries of the camera were completely charged. Those were working fine. He connected the camera to his laptop to check on the memory card. "What! Only 15% memory free, I better delete old files," Ashish said aloud. He opened the files folder and saw 4 new files created about 20 days back. He got up and walked in to Gaurav's room.

"Gaurav, I need you to check these video files which you and Ravi had recorded last. They are taking up most of the space of the memory card and I want to delete them."

'It does not matter, delete them, dad," Gaurav said without even looking up. Ashish could sense that Gaurav wanted to avoid anything which could remind him of his dead friend. He moved closer to Gaurav and caressingly ruffled his hair.

"Check it out once before I delete them," he said soothingly and left the room quietly.

GRAVEYARD SHIFT

Gaurav took the laptop from his father and curled into bed. He looked at the four unnamed files and noticed each had a consecutive date. He clicked on the first one, and the Windows Media Player screen popped up. The frame showed the dark square shape of the apartment on the tenth floor where Gaurav had focused the camera. Soft background sounds were also audible. The length of the video was over 2 hours. Gaurav dragged the pointer slowly fast forwarding through the entire file. The apartment was dark throughout the file. Disinterested, Gaurav closed the window.

"There is nothing in these videos. I will just check the last one"

The video started and likewise before Gaurav cursorily moved the marker forward. At around midway, he slowed down and sat up straight in his bed. Apartment 1003 was no longer dark! It had come alive.

Gaurav quickly paused the video and dragged the marker back to the point where it was all dark. He clicked on the play icon. It began to play.

About ten people lay sleeping next to each other on the open roof top terrace which had been recently constructed, one side of the wall yet to be finished. The twinkling stars and clouded moonlight were enough to illuminate the dark outlines of the snugly sleeping group; a few had also pulled the blankets over their faces. Slowly a figure rose from the group and stood up. It almost looked like an erect shadow. It did not try to remove the blanket which was still wrapped tightly around the body and over the face as well. The person took a few steps forward, closely missing the dozing bodies around. It walked stealthily, slowly, steadily but aimlessly. No one got up, someone turned around but did not wake up. The figure reached the edge of the roof and stood still for a moment. It took a further step forward and disappeared! The blanket flew apart from the falling body which rammed head first on the concrete stone slab below. The skull cracked instantly on impact, the neck twisted with a snap and with a dull thud the body crumpled in a heap of flesh. The blood flowed down in two streams from both the smashed eye sockets. The halogen light from the nearby street lamp fell on the bloodied, disfigured yet youthful face of Ravi Mishra. And then it all went dark. The apartment on the tenth floor was silent yet again.

Betal Pachisi

Foreword:

As far as Indian ghost stories go, there can be little doubt as to which is the most enchanting, most enduring and the most famous ghost story ever written. Betal Pachisi is an epic tale that was originally written in Sanskrit several hundreds of years ago. One of its oldest surviving renditions is in the 12th book of the Katha Sarit Sagara compiled by Maha Kavi Somdev Bhatt, a Saivite Brahmin, in the 11th century. Over the ages, it was first translated into Braj Bhasa, then to Hindi/Hindustani and finally into English in the early nineteenth century, when the British adapted it as a curriculum text book for teaching Hindi to English Sepoys joining the military service.

What I have presented here is my adapted and edited version of the introduction to the original work called Vetal Panchavimshati which focuses on how King Vikramaditya of Ujjaini met and overcame the Vetal. Some paragraphs have been excerpted from Sir Richard Burton's English translation called 'Vikram and the Vampire; or tales of Hindu devilry' dated 1893. A detailed list of sources and references that I have referred to is mentioned in the references at the end of the book.

Children who grew up in the late eighties would remember the television serial 'Vikram Aur Vetal' on Doordarshan featuring the demigod-esque Arun Govil as King Vikram. I still remember getting disappointed and scared every time the hideous looking Vetal slipped away whenever Vikram opened his mouth to speak! I hope the new generation will also get to know and enjoy this wonderful, timeless and classic tale from ancient Indian Literature.

There is one more reason why I have included this adaptation in the book. For that, you need to read the story. Till the very end!

Tathastu.

~~~

130 BCE, Ujjaini, Ancient Bharat

I would have finished that one eyed ogre had it not been for his pet falcon, who – seeing its master's imminent slaughter – dived down from its perch on the cliff and hurtled down towards me. It hit the back of my head like a hammer hitting a nail, its sharp talons piercing my turban and causing seething pain. The one eyed giant, surprisingly did not attempt to overpower me, instead he swiftly threw me off balance and proclaimed in a booming voice:

"O valorous King! Do not kill me. I am Ekanetra, the messenger of the Lord. I was sent to protect your kingdom during your exile."

I had drawn my sword and was about to strike his head down when he said something which made me stop.

"Vikram of Ujjaini," he bellowed, "act like a noble King and I will save you from an impending death. Only listen to the tale which I have to tell you, and use your judgment, and act upon it."

I yelled at Ekanetra, my cries ricocheting across the walls of the mighty hills. "You dare stop me from entering my own kingdom! You dare challenge me for a duel!" "You now dare to even ask me for a pardon."

"Please listen to me so that you may rule in a carefree manner, and live without danger, and die happily," he pleaded.

I considered his words for a moment. Then, although still clutching the hilt of the sharp sword in my hand, I slipped it into its scabbard tied to my waist and gave him a permissive nod to proceed. Ekanetra, the one eyed giant, began narrating his prophecy. I listened, enraptured...

~~~

It was very late in the evening when I finally stood in front of the massive wooden gates of my city, the *dwarpal* immediately prostrating to the ground at the sight of his King. With joyful tears in his eyes, he signalled to the trumpeter standing on the tall watch-post tower, who in turn waved his hands to other men manning the towers circling the entire periphery of the fortified city. Immediately, all the hundreds of trumpeters, in artful unison, sounded a clarion call which pierced through the stillness of the hitherto moribund city; a tune which had not sounded since several years. It was the royal tune only meant for announcing the arrival of the King. Ujjaini and its citizens erupted in unprecedented joy. Musicians deafened the citizens' ears, dancing girls performed till they were about to faint with fatigue. Men abandoned their business, children ran out into the streets, mothers clasping their suckling infants excitedly peered out from their windows, priests clanged the bells of temples, and birds rose in the air; all in solidarity to welcome, greet and meet the King. My heart swelled with pride, just as the eyes welled up with tears of joy. I, their beloved King Vikramaditya, had finally returned.

I did not sleep for the first few days after my return. I was aghast to see my people, my kingdom's state of ruin and atrophy. On my first tour across the city after my return, I observed malnourished children, broken houses, squalid roads, overflowing gutters, empty *gurukulas*, drug peddlers, illicit alcohol dens, pest and rodent-infested granaries and burgled royal treasuries. Without its monarch, there was rampant corruption and fear of law was absent in the citizens' mind. Society had forgotten the moral teachings of our ancient scriptures and the four *varnas* were blatantly inimical to each other. Even the morale of the armed forces was low. The once impregnable borders of my mighty kingdom had become porous due to frequent guerrilla raids by neighbouring warlords. This sorry state of affair troubled me deeply and I did not sleep at all. In fact, I could not.

From the very next day I applied myself unremittingly towards the goal of restoring good governance in administration and eradicating the abuses which had crept into the society. I began to discharge the royal *dharma* of a King and in a month's time Ujjaini was back again on the path of prosperity; ready to reclaim its lost glory as the mightiest empire in whole of *Bharat*. As the seasons changed, so did the state of affairs at Ujjaini. Law and order was restored, children were back to school, commerce started to flourish and my border enemies laid off their nefarious plans. With the arrival of spring, the festival of *Holi* was upon us and I decided to announce a grand celebration across the kingdom. It was amidst this colourful mirth of *Holi* that I first met Shanta Shil.

The faces and dresses of the public were red and yellow with *gulal* and *abir* copiously sprinkled in the festive air as a token of merriment. I had just arrived at my court decked in the best regal attire, attended by several state palanquins glittering with their various ornaments, and escorted by a suite of a hundred kingly personages. To my surprise, the first person waiting to seek my audience was a naked *Aghori*. I was instantly struck by this lean, scraggy little man walking stark naked in my royal court. Being an ardent devotee of Lord Shiva, he had incredibly long dreadlocks – a sign of his extreme asceticism and hardship. He walked up to me, bowed and then offered me a fruit.

I had never seen this fruit before. Its smell was really inviting and the *Aghori* urged me to consume it. I threw a quick glance at my minister, who promptly conveyed to me his disapproval by a firm shake of his head – my enemies might have sent a poisoned fruit to eliminate me. In pursuance of his gesture, I thanked the hermit and gently placed the delicious looking fruit on a golden plate. My guest bowed again and without uttering a single word, turned his back and left the courtroom.

I would have forgotten about this incident and the fruit, but to my inexplicable surprise, the *Aghori* kept coming back to my court every day. On each visit he offered me the same fruit and left without saying anything more than the usual salutations for addressing a King. I was growing more and more suspicious about his intentions and hence never touched the fruit, despite its scrumptious ripe smell. Then one day, while I was sitting in the garden with my queens, I finally discovered the fruit's secret.

My queens were inspecting the gifts, treasures and artefacts which had been accumulating ever since my return. A servant was carrying the golden plate full of fruits given by the *Aghori*. Suddenly, a band of *Langurs* appeared from the nearby thicket making a raucous noise. Seeing the plate laden with ripe fruits, they made a dash for it and began harassing the poor servant, who hurriedly kept the plate on the ground and darted from the garden. I watched the scene, slightly amused. But what I saw next astonished me. The *langurs* snatched the fruits and began devouring them. One by one, they started discarding a stone like substance in place of what should have been the fruit's seed. One of my younger queens ran up to inspect what had emerged from the fruits, and instantly I heard her cry of disbelief. "O King Vikram! Please do come here and see. There lie on the ground hundreds of precious stones, each unmatched in colour, clarity and size."

When the royal lapidary came and inspected the gems, his expression said it all. He confirmed that the value of each stone was far greater than all the treasures in the royal treasury. He said, "Hear, O great king! Each gem is perfect in colour, quality and beauty. If I were to say that the value of each was ten millions of *suvarnas*, even then you would not be able to determine its real worth. In fact, each ruby would buy one of the seven regions into which the earth is divided." Now I was totally puzzled. How could a poor mendicant like the *Aghori* gift me these invaluable gems. I decided to confront him and honour his act of generosity.

The next day when the *Aghori* arrived in the court, I got up from my throne and folding my hands, bowed in front of him. As was the protocol, the whole assembly of royal family, ministers, army commanders, *Brahmins*, teachers, artists also got up and followed me in genuflection. The *Aghori* smiled, looking at me with his piercing eyes. I said "O holy seer, a devotee of Lord Shiva, why did you give me so many pearls, the value of which I cannot even fathom!"

"King Vikram, the blessings of Lord Shiva upon you. I wish to answer your question only in privacy," he replied.

Having heard his request, I escorted him to the private confines of my royal guest house. When we were alone, I asked him "O generous man! You have given me so many rubies, and even for a single day you have not shared food with me; I am exceedingly ashamed, tell me what do you desire?"

"Raja," said the *Aghori*, "My name is Shanta Shil. I am about to perform spells, incantations and magical rites on the banks of the river Godavari, in a large *shamshan*, a cemetery where bodies are burned. I ask you to come and visit me at the eight *prahar* on a specific night and assist me in my ceremony."

I was taken aback at this unexpected request. The *smashana* was a cursed place, certainly not a land where the King should set foot, and definitely not in the unholy hours of the eighth *prahar*. But I was bound by my kingly duties in honouring the wishes of my benefactors, so I agreed to attend the *Aghori*'s occult ceremonies. I inquired when he expected me. Shanta Shil replied coolly.

"You are to come to me alone, armed, but without followers, on the 14th that falls in the dark half of the month *Bhadra*." With that he took his leave.

~~~

In due time the 14th of the dark half of the month *Bhadra* arrived. As the short twilight fell gloomily on earth, I, the warrior king, slipped out unseen through the palace wicket and took the road leading to the *shamshan* on the river bank. Dark and dreary was the night. A heavy thunderstorm was impending; large drops fell in showers from the forest trees as they groaned under the blast, and beneath the gloomy avenue, the clayey ground gleamed ghastly white. As I advanced cautiously, a faint ray of light caught my eyes and directed my footsteps towards the *shamshan*. When I finally reached the open space on the riverbank where corpses were burning, I was shocked at the sight which greeted me.

At the farthest extremity of the *shamshan,* there had gathered an unearthly congregation like which I or anyone else would never have set sight upon. There was an outer circle of hideous bestial forms in which tigers were roaring, elephants were trumpeting, wolves were devouring the remnants of human bodies, foxes, jackals and hyenas were disputing over their prey, whilst bears were savagely chewing the livers of half burnt children. The space within was peopled by a multitude of ghoulish fiends. The subtle bodies of men that had escaped their grosser frames, their corpses having turned to ash, were prowling about the charnel ground. Some were even hovering in the air, waiting till the new bodies which they were destined to animate were made ready for their reception. Vengeful spirits of those that had been unfairly slain wandered about with gashed limbs. The nocturnal air was filled with an obnoxious putrid smell, shrill and strident cries, fitful moaning of the storm-wind and the hoarse gurgling of the swollen river flowing nearby.

GRAVEYARD SHIFT

In the midst of all these, close to the fire which lit up his evil countenance, sat Shanta Shil, the naked *Aghori*, with his magic trident firmly planted in the ground behind him. His black body was striped with lines of chalk, and a girdle of thighbones encircled his waist to hide his private parts. His face was smeared with ashes from a funeral pyre, and his eyes, fixed as those of a statue, shimmered from this mask with an infernal glow of hatred. His cheeks were shaven, and he had not forgotten to draw the horizontal sectarian mark. But that was marked with blood; and as I drew near I saw that he was playing upon a human skull with two shank bones, making music for the horrid revelry.

I drew out my sword and walked up to Shanta Shil. I bowed to him and spoke in a valiant, royal baritone. "O magician of the dark powers, I have come to honour my promise. Tell what can King Vikram do for you?"

"Mighty King, thank you for coming to this unholy place," Shanta Shil said with an evil grin. "About two *kos* away, in a southerly direction, there is another *shamshan*. There you'll find a mimosa tree, on which a body is hanging upside down. Bring it to me immediately."

I was shocked. No, it was not the difficulty of the task that had shaken my senses. It was the recollection of the tale told to me by the one eyed giant Ekanetra whom I had encountered many months ago near the borders of Ujjaini while I was returning from my exile. His peremptory story repeated in my mind, even as I scanned the infernal surroundings where I stood, fires burning with alacrity consuming the mortal remains of once noble men, turning them into ghoulish fiends under the spell of Shanta Shil. I recalled what Ekanetra had said to me – "In short, the history of the matter is that three men were born in this same city of Ujjaini, in the same lunar mansion, and in the same period of time. You, the first, were born in the house of a king. The second was a simple potter, who was slain by the third, a *yogi*. Moreover, the *yogi*, after killing the potter, had suspended him head downwards from a mimosa tree in a cemetery."

I began moving in the direction to which I was set upon. Shanta

Shil resumed beating the skull with renewed vigour. The devilish crowd, which had held its peace during my meeting with Shanta Shil, broke out again in an unrestrained din of whoops and screams, yells and laughter. Two witches crawling on all their fours, tried to impede my path, but I decisively scythed them apart with one swoosh of my sharp sword-blade. But my horrors were only just beginning.

The darkness of the night was frightening, the gloom deepened till it was hardly possible to walk. Lightning blazed forth with an effulgence more than the light of day, and the rumbling roar of the thunder caused the earth to shake. After a lot of trouble walking in squelching mud and dodging snakes and scorpions, I finally arrived at the second *shamshan*. Without much difficulty, I spotted the mimosa tree which in the lightning of the thunder was blazing in a crimson flame. Clutching my sword tightly, I cautiously stepped nearer to the tree and found to my surprise that the fire did not burn me. I stopped and observed the body, which hung, head downwards, from a branch a little above me.

Its eyes, which were wide open, were of a greenish-brown colour, and never twinkled. Its body was thin and ribbed like a skeleton or a bamboo framework and it held on to a bough, like a flying fox, by its toe-tips. The body appeared to have no blood and the only sign of life that it showed was a slowly wagging pointed tail. It was the most hideous and oppressive looking creature I had ever seen. Judging from these signs I at once determined the creature to be a *Betal or Vetal*--a Vampire.

I immediately began climbing the mimosa tree. The *Vetal*, to my surprise, started laughing in a weird manner, seemingly teasing me to come and get him. Wedging my legs firmly between a 'V' shaped joint, formed by queer and uneven growth of the branches, I stretched my hand and with my sword cut the rope from which the *Vetal* lay hanging upside down. He fell to the ground without a thud and before he could flee, I pounced upon him. He did not put up a fight and I swiftly tied his hands and legs with shards of my turban. I looked at him and shouted, "Who are you and why are you hanging from this tree?" No sooner had I spoken, to my utter astonishment, the *Vetal* slipped away and glided smoothly back to his bat like hanging position, all the while laughing hysterically.

I climbed the tree and captured the repulsive creature once more. This time I held him on my back like a rucksack, crumpling him in a bundle with my waistcloth. With a stern voice, I said, "I am Raja Vikramaditya from Ujjaini. Who are you?" Yet again, like before, as soon as I had spoken, the *Vetal* miraculously escaped from my back where I had securely confined him and returned to his former position. This happened at least six or seven times. Every time he would wiggle away no matter how I tried to restrain him. I was nearing exhaustion; it was at my eighth attempt that the vile wretch finally opened his crooked mouth and spoke in a voice which was definitely not human.

"Great warrior King Vikram, I know you have come to take me to that cunning *tantrik* Shanta Shil. I will let you carry me on your back, but I have a condition." *Vetal*'s lips curled into an insincere grin.

"What condition?" Enraged, I bellowed.

"You see, I am a very talkative person and it will take you a couple of hours, given your state of exhaustion, to carry me to Shanta Shil. So to make the journey less tiresome and interesting, I will tell you stories, one after another. At the end of each story, I shall ask you a moral question. If you open your mouth, either due to your conceit of knowing the answer or due to my coaxing, and provide me with the correct answer, I shall immediately fly back to my favourite abode. If you give the wrong answer, I will possess your body and kill you from the inside. Finally, if you keep quiet, I shall stay faithful to you, stay on your back and let you carry me."

I was quite amused by these weird conditions put forward by *Vetal* to get him captured. Ignoring his conditions, I seized the ends of the waistcloth, twisted them into a convenient form for handling. I heaved the bundle inside which he lay, with a jerk and tossed it over my shoulder. I then set off at a round pace towards the western end of the cemetery. The showers had ceased by then, and, as we gained ground, the weather fairly improved. The *Vetal* asked a few indifferent questions about the wind and the rain and the mud. When he received no answer, he began to feel uncomfortable and broke out with these words: "O King Vikram, listen to the true story which I am about to tell you now."

"Once upon a time there was born a beautiful daughter by the name Mandaravati, to a very famous priest. When the daughter grew of age, the father got worried about her marriage. At that time, three eligible bachelors came to her father and each one asked for his daughter's hand. Each of them threatened to kill himself in case the daughter gets married off to any other among the three. The father, however, thought otherwise and decided not to marry her off to anyone of those three."

"One day, she caught a very high pitched fever and died suddenly. All three of them, immensely grief-stricken, cremated the body of their beloved Mandaravati. One of them decided to stay right there and slept on the ashes of Mandaravati. The other took her bones and went to the Ganges. The third became an ascetic and wandered off. On one of his wanderings, the third one reached a *Brahmin*'s house. The *Brahmin*, by the power of a magical spell sprinkled with holy water from the Ganges, was able to bring the dead alive from the ashes. This art of making someone live again was recorded in a book which the *Brahmin* guarded safely. But the third suitor, in the stealth of night, stole that book and went back to the cremation ground of Mandaravati. The second one had by then returned from the Ganges with the holy water, and the first suitor was still there sleeping on the ashes. With the help of the other two, the third suitor then recited the spell from the book and lo! Mandaravati was reborn! Then the three of them started fighting about whose wife she should be; each of them claiming the credit of such revival to his individual effort."

The *Vetal* stopped speaking for a moment and I could feel his cold body wriggle on my back. Then he said in a shrill voice, "O King Vikram, tell me then, which of the three suitors should get to marry Mandaravati?" I thought for a while and said, "The person who brought her back to life by reciting the spell is her creator, it could be her father. The person who took her bones to the Ganges shall be her son. But the person, who committed himself to the ground and slept on her ashes out of love, can be her husband."

At that instant, the *Vetal* broke out in a bout of maniacal laughter and said, "You are correct, but since you have opened your mouth, here I go!" Before I could realize what was happening, the creature effortlessly escaped my harness and flew back to the mimosa tree which we had left quite a far way behind. I uttered a cry of despair and ran back to the tree. There he was, swaying upside down. I began climbing the tree again.

~~~

"Who among the four brothers is responsible for their deaths?" *Vetal* asked. He had finished narrating yet another story and this time I decided to keep mum, although I knew the answer! I said nothing. He kept pestering and coaxing me to speak up but I denied him that wish. But then, that cunning creature of hell scoffed at my deliberate silence as the sign of expected ignorance of a descendant of the royal bloodline of King Gandharvasena, an illustrious member from the house of Paramaras. I would never stand the slightest umbrage upon my forefathers, and I yelled at him furiously.

"O beast, dare not say a word against my clan or my sword will cut you in as many pieces as there are stars above in this night sky."

"You opened your mouth. Here I go!" *Vetal* laughed wickedly. Once again, I felt the touch of coldness vanish from my back as the hideous vampire wriggled free and darted across the sky. Enraged, I ran back to the tree. There he was, swaying upside down. I began climbing the tree once again.

~~~

My lips burnt. I had managed to capture that scoundrel *Vetal* again. He had yet again, for the twenty fourth time recited a parable and posed a confounding question. This time, though, I succeeded in keeping my mouth quiet. I managed this was not because of self-control but because of some clever design, adopted by me.

A few minutes ago, when *Vetal* had escaped from my clutches after tricking me into opening my mouth, I had slumped under a shady tree to take some rest. My arms ached badly and the back muscles were jaded. Before going in pursuit of *Vetal*, I badly needed to quench my thirst and I soon found a gurgling stream nearby. There as I lay resting on my back, my eyes fell upon a file of *moosh pipeelikas* or giant ants scurrying under the bushes. These ants were rare, so rare that sighting them was considered auspicious. They were of the size of a small mouse and had razor sharp fangs which could deliver an unbearable nasty bite. During my wanderings, I had once encountered a *vaidya* stitching the open wounds of a soldier using these *moosh pipeelika's* fangs. Holding the viciously angry ant by its neck, he made the ant bite into the skin on both sides of the gash. Then the *vaidya* deftly cut off the fangs leaving them embedded in the skin where the ant had bit. Sight of these extraordinary ants had given me an idea. I sutured my lips the same way I had seen the *vaidya* stitching the open wound. Just one bite from the ant was enough to clamp down my lips. The mild venom, transmitted through the fangs, caused those to swell slightly, further shutting my mouth completely. After the initial spasms of pain had subsided, I had quickly pulled myself to my feet and wrapped a cloth around my face, covering my mouth and leaving just enough slit wide open around my eyes. Then I set off to fetch my ghoulish quarry.

The beast on my back did all he could to get me to speak out. He provoked me, he slyly coaxed me, and he even insulted my queen! But I kept quiet, rather the ant's fangs held on firmly. Finally, he relented and said in a praiseworthy voice:

"O valorous king of Ujjaini! You have kept quiet and I am impressed. I shall now keep my side of the promise and allow you to carry me to Shanta Shil, but be prepared to listen to something carefully which I am about to tell you, your majesty."

"Three men were born in the holy city of Ujjaini, in the same lunar mansion and in the same period of time. It was ordained that only one of those three would go on to acquire immense power, prestige, wealth and a long life. You, the first, were born in the house of a king. The second one was me, a simple potter. The third was the ascetic Shanta Shil who killed me and condemned me to this execrable existence. He is now plotting to sacrifice you at the altar of the goddess Kali and thereby claim the prophecy for himself. Be wise, O great King, heed my words and act accordingly." With that *Vetal* fell silent.

I had been listening attentively to what *Vetal* said. His was the same story which the giant Ekanetra had also told me. It all was clear to me now. I had been tricked by that *Aghori*. It was now time to finish this business once and for all. I hastened my steps in the direction of the *shamshan*. There was Shanta Shil, dressed in his usual habit, a deerskin thrown over his back, and twisted reeds instead of a garment hanging round his loins. The hair had fallen from his limbs and his skin was bleached ghastly white as a consequence of constant exposure to the elements. A fire seemed to exude from his mouth. He was drumming upon a skull, and exclaiming vociferously, "Ho Kali! Ho Durga! Ho *Devi*!"

Likewise before, strange beings were holding their wild carnival in Shanta Shil's presence. As I entered the burning-ground, the tall gaunt trees groaned aloud, bowed and trembled like slaves bending before their master Shanta Shil! At times, the dull gurgling of the swollen river was heard in the distance, interrupted by rumbling sounds of explosions, as chunks of loosened earth from the banks fell headlong into the stream. But once the *Aghori* raised his arm, everything around became still. The nature lay breathless, as if asphyxiated under the effect of his powerful and ominous spells.

I briskly strode up to Shanta Shil and dropped the bundle from my back. I unwrapped the cloth and exposed to Shanta-Shil's glittering eyes the corpse, which had now recovered its proper form -- that of a young potter. Seeing it, Shanta Shil was delighted and thanked me, extolling my immense courage and fearless daring efforts, rating those above any other monarch that had yet lived. He pulled out a sharp scythe and dismembered the corpse's head, holding it by its hair and letting the dripping blood collect in a small bowl; all the while repeating certain charms and *mantras* facing the fire. He emptied the blood filled bowl over his head and eagerly offered to the fire: betel leaf and flowers, sandal wood and unbroken rice, fruits, and the flesh extracted from the corpse's stomach. Lastly, he filled the skull in his hand with burning embers, blew upon them till they shot forth tongues of crimson light, serving as a lamp, and then motioned me to follow him. I knew where he was leading me – to the temple of Goddess Kali! I followed him silently.

We passed through the quadrangular outer court of the temple whose piazza hung in a deep shade. We circled the small central shrine in complete silence, and every time Shanta Shil struck the bell three times, it gave forth a loud and ominous clang. Finally after five such ritualistic rounds, Shanta Shil stepped over the threshold and looked into the gloomy inner depths. There stood *Smashana*-Kali, the goddess, in her most horrid form. She was a black deity with half-severed head, partly cut and partly painted, resting on her shoulder; and her tongue lolled out from her wide yawning mouth. She was robed in an elephant's hide, dried and withered, confined at her waist with a belt composed of hands and limbs of the giants whom she had slain in war. She wore a necklace beaded with bleached skulls. She stood with one leg on the breast of her husband, Shiva, while the other on his thigh. Before the idol lay utensils and various other paraphernalia of worship. I knew the time was near when Shanta Shil would make his move. I felt my pulse rising and my heart thumped louder.

"Let prosperity be bestowed upon you forever and ever, O mighty Vikram!" exclaimed Shanta Shil, after he had muttered a prayer before the image. "You have rightfully redeemed your pledge, and by the virtue of your presence all my wishes shall presently be accomplished. Look to the east, the sun is about to rise over the distant hills, and your task now ends. Please prostate before the Goddess Kali, and be blessed by her."

I deliberately obeyed Shanta Shil's instruction, knowing very well what was coming. Before the bludgeoning axe could fall on my neck, I instinctively rolled over, drew out my faithful sword in one swift motion, and yanked out Shanta Shil's head from his torso. His headless body quivered for a moment and then crashed to the stone floor. At the same instant the image of Goddess Kali also fell with the sound of thunder upon the floor of the temple. The nightmare was over. Shanta Shil was dead. I bowed to the rising sun and chanted the *Gayatri Mantra* with aplomb.

Suddenly I heard a heavenly voice from the sky above saying: "A man is justified in killing someone who has the desire to kill him." Then glad shouts of triumph and victory were heard from all directions. They came from the celestial courtiers, the heavenly dancers, the mistresses of the gods, and the nymphs of Indra's Paradise. At last the brilliant god of gods, Indra himself, with thousand eyes, rising from the shade of the heavenly *Parijat* tree, appeared in his divine chariot drawn by seven golden yellow steeds. His attendants sounded the heavenly drums and rained a shower of flower blossoms and perfumes. Lord Indra asked me a boon. In joy and gratitude I fell to the ground and said respectfully:

"O the mighty ruler of the lower firmament, let this story of my adventurous encounter with Shanta Shil and *Vetal* become famous throughout the world!"

"*Tathastu*," re-joined Indra. "As long as the sun and moon will continue their celestial existence and shine and the sky continues to look down upon the ground, shall your adventure will be told and retold for centuries after you are gone." With that his heavenly chariot ascended towards the skies and disappeared among the clouds. I cleaned my sword of the blood smear and gleefully started walking back to Ujjaini.

REFERENCES

While writing these tales, I have done a lot of research. Given below is a list of resources which I have referred

Tales in the Train
1. http://en.wikipedia.org/wiki/Churel
2. http://www.paranormalresearchsocietyofindia.com/Haunted%20Locations.html
3. About Chhalava http://www.avdhessharya.com/paranormal-phenomenon-the-dark-and-scary-side-of-life/
The Last Wish
4. http://en.wikipedia.org/wiki/Lalgarh_Palace
5. http://en.wikipedia.org/wiki/Laxmi_Vilas_Palace,_Vadodara
Honey, 'm Back
6. http://www.naturetrails.in/Dabhosa.html
A Doll named Wendy
7. http://www.tribuneindia.com/1998/98dec06/sunday/head2.htm
8. http://en.wikipedia.org/wiki/Bhangarh
A Night in Hastings House
9. http://en.wikipedia.org/wiki/Warren_Hastings
10. http://en.wikipedia.org/wiki/Impeachment_of_Warren_Hastings
11. http://en.wikipedia.org/wiki/Belvedere_Estate
12. http://www.bartleby.com/268/6/3.html
13. Beneath (Novel) by Kit Tinsley.
14. http://www.tribuneindia.com/2000/20000122/windows/main4.htm
15. http://kolkataonwheelsmagazine.com/kolkata-news/news-flash/what-haunts-kolkatas-haunted-houses/
16. http://www.funeralhelper.org/popular-a-prayer-for-the-dead.html
17. "A Complete Guide to Black Magic &The Occult" Part II "How to Conduct a Séance" By: Abdul Alhazred
18. http://www.museumoftalkingboards.com/directio.html
19. "How to use an Ouija Board" http://www.youtube.com/watch?v=h3u37yV9wQo
Betal Pachisi
20. http://www.sacred-texts.com/goth/vav/vav04.htm
21. http://www.sacred-texts.com/goth/vav/vav16.htm
22. http://8ate.blogspot.in/2009/10/baital-pachisi-twenty-five-tales-of.html
23. http://www.arshavidyacenter.org/OLD/purnavidya/betal.pdf

24. http://en.wikipedia.org/wiki/Baital_Pachisi
25. https://archive.org/details/baitlpachsortwe00forbgoog

Glossary

Some storiesuse colloquial terms from Hindi language to enhance the narrative impact by giving the tales an Indian earthy feel. Presented below are a few terms and their meanings

Tales in the Train
Chacha: Uncle
Sarpanch: the village headman
Chaaai…garam chaai: Tea…hot tea

A Doll named Wendy
Almirah: Cupboard
Tantrik: Black Magician
Haveli: Mansion
Chhatri: Minaret

The Last Wish
Sarkari Babu: Government Officer
Fakir: Hermit
Shaitaan: Satan

Betal Pachisi
Dwarpal: Gate keeper
Gurukul: Boarding school during ancient times
Varnas: The four castes in Hindu society
Dharma: Moral religion
Gulal & Abir: Coloured powder used in Holi
Aghori: Ascetic practicing a form of extreme penance and/or dark arts
Langur: Species of monkey
Suvarna: Gold pieces
Smashana: Place where last rites of Hindus are performed
Prahar: Ancient unit of time. Day divided into 8 prahars starting at 3:00 AM
*Bhadra:*6th month of the Hindu calendar
Kos: Ancient unit of distance between 1.8kms to 3.2 kms
Yogi: Hermit
Moosh Pipeelika: Giant ant (fictional does not exist in reality)
Vaidya: Doctor or Medic

ABOUT THE AUTHOR

Manish is a consulting professional with international experience in big and small corporations. He currently lives in Mumbai with his wife Pratima and son Viaan.

Born and brought up in the east, Manish is actually from the west, has lived in the south and talks like someone from the north. These pan Indian experiences flow into his writing and his stories are built upon cultural milieu from rural and urban India. His debut book "The Disappearance of Tejas Sharma...and other Hauntings: Ghost Stories from India" was published in 2013 and was well received.

In his youth, Manish was heavily interested in Greek mythology and had serious delusions of being a Greek god. Then on a summer afternoon, things changed. He heard the song 'The Number of the Beast' by Iron Maiden and realized that ghastly ghouls are more interesting than Greek gods. Today, he would just shrug off the fact that his cell phone number ends with a 666!

Wrapping a live adult Burmese python around his neck in Malaysia, surviving a 3 month stint in Saudi Arabia, swallowing a sea cucumber in China, watching the sun rise over Mt. Lantang in Nepal, visiting the Great Pyramid of Giza in Egypt and losing all money at the roulette in Macao are a few highlights of his otherwise dull life. Outside his passion of writing, he maintains a lively bucket list of unfulfilled dreams. His eyes which see such vivid dreams are pledged and he would encourage everyone to do so as well.

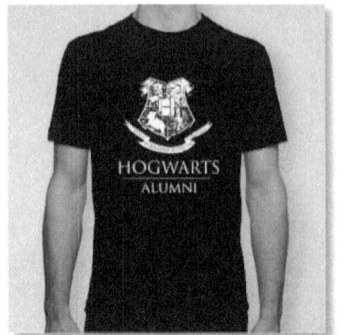

If you're a movie buff or love watching television shows, you can buy merchandise of your favourite movie/TV series at a discounted price NOW.

Just log on to **greenrockstore.com** and use the coupon code '**ROCK20**' to avail **discount** up to **20%**.

Other Titles by Half Baked Beans

Available on Amazon and Flipkart

YAMA
Kevin Missal

All I Need is you
MUKUND VERMA

KALIYUG
The Secret Plot
B.S.Sarwagna Kumar

NO TIME TO PAUSE
Pavithra Ramesh

SCARLET NIGHTS
MAYUR PATEL

tagged
M Kaarthika Santhosh

WILD CARD
Asfiya Rahman

THE INDIAN AMERICAN DREAM
PRANAY SAHU

Thank You Love..
"Taking love beyond words"
Ayush Gupta

www.ingramcontent.com/pod-product-compliance
Lightning Source LLC
Chambersburg PA
CBHW030255130626
46549CB00002B/544